From Terror To Glory

A Family's Attack by the Demonic Realm and How Jesus Christ Set Them Free

Susan Knauff

Copyright © 2003 by Susan Knauff

From Terror To Glory
by Susan Knauff

Printed in the United States of America

Library of Congress Control Number: 2002117061
ISBN 1-591604-18-4

All rights reserved. No part of this publication may be reproduced or transmitted in any form or by any means without written permission of the publisher.

Unless otherwise indicated, Bible quotations are taken from The Holy Bible, New King James Version, Copyright © 1979, 1980, 1982, Thomas Nelson Inc., Publishers.

Xulon Press
10640 Main Street
Suite 204
Fairfax, VA 22030
(703) 934-4411
XulonPress.com

To order additional copies, call 1-866-909-BOOK (2665).

Dedication

Dedicated to Margo Bock and Stefan Bock, and Michelle, for pointing out the way to freedom. You have blessed us so very much. Your burning desire for serving the Lord and your love of soaking in His presence caused us to seek more of Him, ourselves. What a blessed family we have!

Dedicated to Terry and Bobby Grapenthin, for their love of the Father and their obedience to Him. Thank you for coming to us in love, during our time of need. Thank you for showing us how to worship Him, pressing in and seeking Him, until the glory falls!

Dedicated to my Father in Heaven and my Savior, Jesus Christ. Lord, thank You for your loving forgiveness. Thank You for setting my family free. Thank You for showing me Your glory! Knowing You personally Lord, hearing Your voice and seeing Your signs, wonders, and miracles… I can't thank you enough, Lord. I love You Jesus. You led us through the wilderness and there is glory on the other side!

Prelude

How many of us have heard the infamous ghost story as a child and even enjoyed being frightened a bit as children as we listened to these tales? That was my childhood and many hours were spent under the neighborhood streetlight sharing these tales of darkness.

I remember as a child hearing those scary stories and being very frightened yet as I matured I wanted to know more and hear more. Was this just innocent childhood fun? Some would say so.

After what I have been through in my lifetime, I can tell you it is not innocent. It is a drain that slowly begins to twirl, and then more rapidly as time passes, it spins you, and then finally, it pulls you under. However, I found a way out of that drain. The Lord Jesus Christ saved my entire family. We were literally ripped out of darkness and shown the light.

As you read my story, please understand that while it starts out as a child unknowingly delving into some occult activities, it ends with victory for our Lord and Savior Jesus Christ.

I write my story to make others aware of the fact that some sleepover games that children are playing are, unfortunately, actually opening the doors to allow satan into their lives. I pray parents read this and talk with their children as soon as they can about these types of games.

I write my story in the hopes that others who have always "sensed more" in the spirit realm, come to use their gifts in a way that God would have them to use them.

I write my story to help the family that goes to bed in fear at night, because of an unseen force in their home. You are not alone in what you are experiencing and there is help for you that works. You will find help through authority in Jesus Christ! Read on…

Contents

Dedication v

Prelude vii

Chapter One: Childhood Fears, Games and Concerns 11

Chapter Two: Why Is This Happening To Me? 23

Chapter Three: Terror 41

Chapter Four: I Will Lift Up Mine Eyes Unto The Hills
From Whence Cometh My Help 67

Chapter Five: Glory 81

CHAPTER ONE

Childhood Fears, Games and Concerns

I grew up in the typical family with my mother and father and older sister. I remember having unusual spiritual insight as a child. I never knew why, but I often saw or felt things that others did not see.

As an infant I was placed on a type of sedative so that my mother could sleep because I cried constantly. I would panic if she tried to lay me on my back to change my diaper. I remember many nights as a child waking up in fear. Fear that I would die or fear that something was going to happen to me. My mother began to dread the nights because I always woke her up and begged her to sit with me as I shook and trembled in fear. I didn't know where these fears came from but they were with me from as early on as I can remember.

The first incident occurred when I was about 6 years old. My parents woke me before dawn one morning to tell me that we were about to take a 14-hour drive, from Ohio to Arkansas to visit family. I usually didn't mind the trips but on this one particular morning I began to sense fear in me like I'd never known. I began to cry and tell my mother that I didn't want to go because something bad was going to happen. She said I'd just been awakened too early. I wanted her to heed my words so badly and yet she wouldn't.

We were about half way into the drive on the interstate when while talking on the CB radio my father didn't see a patch of ice on the road and the car went into a spin. I remember sleeping in the back seat and waking up to the sound of the tires screeching and looking up to see my father struggling with the wheel, pulling it back and forth and back and forth, as we were hit again and again by cars unable to stop behind us. When we finally came to a stop near the side of the road, my father checked to see we were all ok and then got out of the car to check on the other vehicles involved. I looked at my mother and said, "I told you this was going to happen." She just looked at me in amazement, turned to my sister and said, "She did. Didn't she?"

We all escaped that horrible car accident mainly uninjured except for my mother, who had scraped her knees on the CB equipment mounted in front of her, and my father who had bumped his head on the steering wheel.

When I was about 8 or 9 years of age, my parents were going away one evening and my sister was asked to watch over me. We stayed the evening with friends down the street. My parents gave us the key to get into the house should we need to. My sister and her friend were baking a cake and needed some cinnamon. She asked me to walk back to my house with her friends' younger sister, who was about 3 years older than me, to get some cinnamon from mom's kitchen. As we walked the short distance down the road, the sun was just setting in the sky. As we came near my house we could see the entire street was lined with old cars, from the 1940's era. We wondered together in amazement at where they had all come from. We came to my house and in the field next to the house there was a strange man and woman walking my dog and looking up at us smiling as though they were happy to see us. They were dressed as though they'd just gotten married. She was in a very old fashioned wedding gown and he was dressed in a tuxedo and top hat. Yet they wore clothes like I'd never seen before. I began to get frightened. My friend saw them too. I said, "That's my dog! Who are those people?" We looked at my house where every light was on in every room inside and you could see quite a few people walking around on the inside, passing the windows. I wondered if my parents had brought some people home with them and didn't tell us they were back yet. I couldn't locate their car at all. I said that to my friend who just stood there, staring and suggesting that we should leave. I became very frightened at that point and said, "Lets just go get my sister!" We turned and ran.

We opened the door to my friends' house and very winded,

began to ask them to hurry and come see this. They didn't know what was wrong and all that I could say was people are in our house and walking our dog outside. My sister and my friends' older sister then immediately came with us. No more than 4 or 5 minutes could have passed before we got down the road to my street. The old cars were entirely gone and so were all of the people and our house was dark inside. They laughed at us and said we had wonderful imaginations. I knew what I'd seen was real yet unexplainable. I thought I'd literally stepped back in time. I was frightened and so was my friend.

My parents returned home that night only to hear my bizarre story and although they seemed concerned at first, they dismissed it. Yet it was a proven fact that they hadn't returned home earlier that evening and to their knowledge no one had been there.

My friend and I spent many hours talking about what we'd seen that day. Even as we grew older, our stories never changed and were identical. Yet that day was never explained. It remained a mystery.

My childhood was spent with many sleepless nights and many nights of sleepwalking and horrible dreams.

The time came when my sister was driving. She was seven years older than me. I remember her excitement one day as she was given permission to drive to the grocery store in our brand new, baby blue Pontiac. I was allowed to go along as well.

As she pulled into the very busy parking lot, I remember thinking to myself, "I feel like she is going to get into an accident. Not a big accident, but a little one that doesn't hurt anyone." I kept telling myself, "Don't think like that!"

My sister was driving down an isle and a car was coming right at her so she tried to pull out of the way by pulling into a tiny parking space. She scratched the side of the Pontiac. I looked at her and said, "I knew that was going to happen."

Times like that one didn't thrill me. It felt very creepy to me that I had this forewarning knowledge. I didn't want it. I didn't like it.

I remembered as kids my sister and I would play this game where she would get a deck of playing cards and lay one on my forehead, face down. She'd ask me to take my time and try and guess what the card was. She was shocked at the times that I actually did know what card and suit it was.

By the time I entered high school, I was much more settled down. I had decent grades and was involved in band and the flag corp. I had many friends and was sleeping now through the night. Life felt good.

My circle of friends had many sleepovers and one of the popular things to do was to play with the Oijia Board and ask it silly questions or to work at trying to get a friend to relax and lift them from a table with each person around them using only one finger.

I remember one night in particular that we all began to rub our temple area because someone said it would produce a trance like state. We all felt nothing spectacular but when we decided to stop trying, one girl was just staring and we were unable to bring her out of it. She would stare and not respond. She would stand up and walk with us but there was no expression on her face. We walked her to her mother's house and left her in her mothers' care saying that we thought for sure she must be faking it. She was back in school a day later. All of us doubted her sincerity, that night, but I often wondered if something more had happened to her. She never again mentioned that night.

What frightened me the most though, was a particular thing that one group of friends used to try to get me to do. We were to look in a mirror and say 13 times repeatedly the name of Mary Worth. I did not know where this name came from, but I was told if I was brave enough to say it that either I might see her in the mirror and that she was very ugly with worms for hair or I'd wake up in the morning with scratches on my face. Many times I refused and then I remember one night bravely saying the name, counting out each time. Nothing happened, yet during the night we woke up to hear the back door open and heavy footsteps walk in the house and down the basement steps. We were three girls home alone (as their parents both worked nights) and we ran together in terror to lock the basement door.

We called my friends' mother, all the while crying hysterically, and she called the police who came out and found no one inside the house or basement. We stayed awake all night long until her parents returned home early in the morning. Only later on in life was I to realize the full extent of what our little game in the mirror meant.

Childhood Fears, Games and Concerns

In my 10th year of high school a close friend of mine came over one evening and we lit candles and went into my kitchen and got out the Ouijja board. We began to ask it questions. Our high school basketball team was going to state finals and we wanted to know if it could tell us who would win. We asked it repeatedly and it ignored our question but would spell out a young mans name that I didn't know. I asked my friend if she knew this young man and she said no. We went on to ask other questions when the board suddenly became very active and spelled out many things to us. It spelled out: 11:50 PM, car accident, radio. My friend became very frightened saying that she was driving to the state finals and was worried that it meant she would get in a car accident. I was taking a bus down with several other classmates and the timing did concern me, as well. We quickly put the board away and said that was enough.

State finals for our high school basketball team came and went uneventfully with no problems. My friend phoned me the day after to tell me that she had driven home and had pulled into her driveway at 11:45 PM thankful that she wasn't on the road at that time. Our bus trip went smoothly as well. We wrote off the silly boards' words… until… a few weeks later.

I was walking down the hall in school when my friend came up to me and said, "Guess what?" She said, "I remember who the name that the board spelled out is!"

I said, "What are you talking about?"

She said, "The name, that neither one of us knew, that night at your house… with the Ouijja board?"

I responded, "Oh, you know that guy?" She said, "Yes! I thought of it only after his parents called my parents the other day! His parents are friends with my parents, but I hadn't thought of him in years."

I just assumed that her mind kept the name and it subconsciously came out while she was playing with the board. I never believed in the thing really anyway… until… a few weeks later.

I was sitting in class when my friend came up to me and said, "You aren't going to believe this! He died!"

I said, "Who?"

She said, "The guy that the board named. He died last night in a car crash."

I said, "Oh I'm so sorry to hear that."

She grabbed me and said, "Remember? REMEMBER? The things the board spelled out? CAR CRASH… 11:50 PM… RADIO?"

I said, "YES! OH NO!"

She said, "He died last night at 11:50 PM. He was driving too fast and they say he must have been looking down, switching radio stations and missed the curve. He went off the road. He died!"

My mouth fell open in horror. I threw the Ouijja board away that afternoon when I got home. I put it right into the trash. I was so frightened that whatever we had tapped into on the so-called, "other side", that it knew when someone would die. I didn't want a thing like that anywhere near me, ever again.

Somehow I felt ashamed that I hadn't known to put it all together or that I didn't notify that family. I felt ashamed that I'd even played with this board that would tell us something like that. It was awful and it felt evil.

One day my family had received word that my grandfather, on my father's side of the family, was very ill and that we needed to get there as soon as possible. The doctors didn't know if he would make it until we got there. We packed up for the long drive to Arkansas. However, on the way there, it was my grandmother, his wife, who suddenly passed away at home. It was a very sad time for my family.

When we arrived, my parents went to the hospital to visit my grandfather. Words just can't explain how hard this was on the entire family. As my parents went to the hospital, they left me in my grandparents' home in the care of my uncle. As he lie down on the couch and switched on the television set, I went off to a spare bedroom. There was a very high bed in that room and I always loved to lie on top of it and read my grandmothers magazines. She loved reading the ones that featured the true stories of peoples' lives. I did too. I crawled up on that high bed with magazines gathered up around me and began to read.

A few minutes later I sensed a presence enter the room. I turned expecting to see my uncle coming to check in on me. There was no one there. I tried to go back to reading and the feeling became more intense. I literally felt the hair stand up on the back of my neck in response to my growing fear. I tried to ignore it. There was a very old antique dresser in the corner of the room that I always loved to sit at and stare into the old fogged up glass mirror on it. For some reason I felt this presence somehow guiding me to look at the mirror. I would not look up and grew more afraid of what I would see if I did. I turned the other direction and ran out of that room, sitting in the living room instead, with my uncle the rest of the night.

Later, I was certain that it was my grandmother paying me a final visit. It was comforting to think that is what I had felt and sensed in that room. It was how I explained it all away. Again, only later would I realize what really tried to pay me a visit that night.

Again, I shared this story with my parents and they would just laugh at a little girls imagination. Even as I write these words, I can see why they thought that it was just that… my imagination. I can only say that as time went on in my life, many more things were revealed to me.

My grandfather upon hearing the news of his wife's death, grieved so hard and wept openly and loudly. They had married very young while in their teens and had been married until they were in their 80's. It was very hard to see him suffer that way.

He lapsed into a coma and all of his organs began shutting down, one by one. His skin turned orange from his kidney's failing and he literally became stiff as though dead already. The doctors said it would be any moment now. We waited. We gathered with family and held hands and prayed for him in that hospital hallway. It was a long night. Morning came and I heard my mother laughing in his room. I walked in to find him sitting up and saying, "I'm hungry." It was a miracle! The doctors couldn't believe it. He was stiff, they kept saying. My grandfather said, "I saw the Lord and He told me that I had to go back home for awhile. He said it wasn't time for me yet and I should go home for another year or so." My dear grandfather passed away almost a year after that.

CHAPTER TWO

Why Is This Happening To Me?

I fell in love with a young man from high school, that I had dated for one year, and we married, already expecting a baby, at the young age of 17. We were supported and helped by our parents until we finished high school and had an apartment of our own.

I had given birth to a beautiful baby girl. As time went on, I realized that something was wrong with my baby. She would suddenly develop a fixated stare and make strange mouthing movements and her lips would turn blue momentarily. These episodes could last up to 3 minutes and then she would be fine again.

I went from physician to physician explaining the symptoms. I was told that I was too young of a mother and my baby was fine and healthy. I finally found one pediatrician who agreed to put her into the hospital for observation. As my little one slept in the hospital crib and another episode began I ran to get a nurse into the room.

She took notes and vital signs and finally I had someone professional witness what I had been seeing all along.

The pediatrician referred us to a local neurologist who came in and told us that my baby was having petit mal seizures and that they would put her on some medications for it and possibly she would outgrow them as she matured. It was hard to swallow this news, but I was glad there was an answer and that she would be fine one day. His final recommendation to us was that we get a routine cat scan before we left the hospital, just to rule out anything else and that we see him within a few days in his office, for follow up.

They sedated our baby to keep her still for the cat scan. I sat in a dark waiting room with my husband while the test was being conducted. It was a long wait. I heard her pediatrician being paged to come to the x-ray department. I knew this didn't mean good news.

The doctor somberly entered the waiting room and sat down and said suddenly and bluntly, "Your daughter has a brain tumor. It is located deep inside the brain. It is inoperable. As this tumor grows, well,'" he said, "she will more than likely not live another full year."

I burst into tears. I remember the doctor leaning over me and for some reason I thought he was seeking to comfort me and put his arm around my shoulders. I reached out to hug someone, anyone. Instead he removed my arm from his and placed the tissue box that he had been reaching for, into my hand, and casually walked out of the room.

My mother and sister were waiting in the hallway. I looked at my husband who just sat there in shock over the hurtful news. I ran out to my mom and told her and they both began to cry and I watched as my mother sunk to the floor with the shock of it all. I went back in the room to my husband and we held each other and cried.

They placed our sleeping little one in our arms and we sat there, so devastated. We cried, looking at her peaceful face. I remember thinking that this could not be. She looked fine and healthy.

As they placed her in a rolling crib and wheeled her down the hallway back to her room, I felt the full sheer terror of what had just been said to me. I began to pace and cry and say over and over again, no, no, no. I was always afraid of medications, but I looked at my mother and said I'm not going to be able to handle this. I asked her if she could get me some nerve pills. She phoned my doctor and went to get the prescription for me and handed me one with a glass of water. I don't remember who called my husbands parents but they were there in the room as well. We all cried and cried. I remember wondering why no one was hugging me or comforting me during this time. Everyone was just hurting so much in his or her own way, I guess. I saw my husband in a chair crying. My mom came to me and said, "You need to go comfort him." I just thought but…what about me? However I turned and went to him and sat on his lap and wrapped my arms around him. We cried and I looked up and thought, 'Lord help us." I knew about Jesus and mom had taught me about the Bible stories and sent me on the bus to Sunday school. Though we weren't a church attending family, I had given my heart to Jesus, when I was very young. So my mind called out to Him, for help. I had nowhere else to go and no one to turn to.

It was then that I heard the Lord and His trueness and His surety. I heard it somehow, and I knew somehow that it was in my spirit that He had spoken.

I looked up and said, "She's going to be fine!" They all stared at me. I said, "No, I know it! She's going to be fine. She will be! She's going to make it!" They all looked sympathetically at me as though I was just saying it to feel better. I said, "She will live! She will!"

We left the hospital with the grim news and a slip of paper referring us to the Cleveland Clinic Foundation where perhaps they could offer us a bit more help with our baby's situation.

We were seen by some of the top neurologists at the Cleveland Clinic and told that perhaps this tumor would not grow at all and that the doctors as a group had conferred and decided to just do routine cat scans and watch it closely. In the meantime, they placed our daughter on seizure medication to control her seizures.

We went through probably 4 different types of seizure medications. Some made her too drowsy. Another would cause hyperactivity. Another caused severe crying and mood swings. They placed her on the 4th medication and the doctor said he hoped this one worked as there wasn't much left for a child her age to try. If her seizures continued, I was to call them and they would raise the dosage.

Her seizures continued and the dosage that was being given to her was incredible. It was not working. I was getting discouraged.

I remember one night, after she'd had a seizure, I put her to bed and knelt down beside her watching her while she slept. I bowed my head and began to pray to ask Jesus into my heart once again, knowing that I hadn't prayed to the Lord in such a long time. I raised my head and looked out her little bedroom window and saw the stars. I thought of God's greatness and cried out to Him desperately. I said, "Lord please don't punish my child because I've been bad. I would take the seizures myself, would you give them to me. I've taken her to the best doctors there is. I've done all I can physically do, Lord. I can do no more, here for her. Humanly possible, I can do no more. Please help her." Then a thought came to my mind and it was frightening to me. I prayed this anyway, frightened at what the Lord would do, but I said, "Lord, I fully give my child to you. I can't stand to see her suffer any longer, Lord. Lord I can do no more. I trust You though. If she were with You, in heaven, she'd have a better life than here, but I pray You don't take her, Lord. I pray instead that You heal her and take the seizures and tumor away. Please Lord. She is all Yours." I cried immensely after that. I didn't want the Lord to take her from me, yet I didn't want her to suffer. I was frightened and had only Him to turn to. I knew He loved my little girl though. He created her.

A few days later, I put my daughter in the car and I picked up my sister in law to go shopping at a local shopping mall. It was early morning and the mall wasn't crowded at all. We walked around, pushing my daughter in the stroller and she began to fall asleep as we walked. We were laughing and enjoying the day together, when we looked up and noticed a young girl up ahead of us. She seemed to be standing there waiting for us.

This young girl seemed to be around 14 yrs of age and very plain looking. By that, I mean that nothing stood out about her. She had a very plain hairstyle and clothing. She was standing up ahead and staring right us and smiling. As we walked further and drew near to her, my sister in law and I looked at each other and began to smile too, wondering what the young girl wanted.

This young girl put up her hand as though to say, "stop" to us. We looked at each other puzzled. We stopped and she motioned to us by covering her mouth and then her ears and shaking her head no, that she couldn't speak or hear. My sister in law said, "I don't think she can speak or hear." I said, "Oh, my." We smiled at her. The young girl put her arms in a rocking a baby, motion. Then she pointed at my daughter. I looked at my sister in law who said, "I think she wants to hold her." I was afraid and looked around to see if this young girl had any parents with her. I saw no one close by. Again, the girl motioned that she wanted to hold my daughter and smiled at me. I unbuckled my daughter and handed her over to the girl. She seemed so joyous to hold her in her arms. She gazed at my child's sleeping face. Then this young girl placed her hand over her own heart and then onto my daughter's head. She did this several times. Then she handed her back to me and waved goodbye to us. We just laughed and smiled with her.

She stood there while I settled my daughter back into her stroller and as I stood up, she waved goodbye to us. I waved goodbye as well. We took two steps to leave and I immediately said to my sister in law, "That was strange. Where are her parents?" She said, "I was thinking the same thing!" We turned around to wave goodbye and the young girl was gone. She had no time to get into a store. We were in the middle of the mall hallway. It was not crowded. She couldn't have gotten lost in the crowd. I said, "She's gone!" I looked at my sister in law and saw the expression on her face. We left the mall without saying much to one another at all on the way home.

It was only a few weeks later that she and I spoke about that incident that day and she said she honestly felt we had been visited by an angel of the Lord. I felt the same thing the minute the girl disappeared in the middle of the mall.

Amazingly, my daughters' seizures stopped right after that. The doctors said the medications must have finally worked. I knew differently. God was taking care of her now.

During the early years of my marriage and while raising my little girl, we lived in a duplex. We had the upstairs part of a very old house. My husband would leave for work early in the morning and I would get up and start my day. Many mornings while eating breakfast, I'd hear footsteps coming down the attic steps. I always kept the door to the attic locked and we never went up there. The sound I heard nearly every morning though was just unmistakable. I would get my daughter dressed early and we would go outside to play most of the day. When my husband came home and would check for me, there was never anyone up there or anyway that anyone could have gotten up there. I began to fear when it came time for him to leave again.

One morning after he left, the footsteps began again. A distinct thump, thump, as I listened. When I knew they'd reached the bottom of the steps, I'd looked over to see the door handle slowly turning. I panicked. I grabbed my daughter up out of bed and dressed her quickly. I packed a bag of drinks and snacks and we left walking. My mother lived 10 - 15 minutes away by car and I thought for sure we could walk that far. I didn't have a phone to call anyone to come and get me.

I walked so far, letting my daughter walk as much as she could and then picking her up and carrying her. It was getting hot and I had carried her so much that I didn't think I could go on much longer. I saw a man outside watering his lawn and asked if I could use his phone. He kindly let me in and I called my mother to come and get us. She hurried down to pick us up, saying she couldn't believe we had walked as far as we did. I told her I was so frightened of what I'd heard and seen. She told me it was probably the stairs contracting as the sun came up that morning and warmed them and the attic. I wanted to believe that. However, the next time

I heard it, I knew it was too loud, heavy and distinct to be a creaking of stairs. Soon the downstairs apartment became available and we were able to rent that. Downstairs, I never experienced anything strange or out of the way.

We had begun attending church regularly with my mother in law. It was a small Baptist church and I felt very welcomed there. An evangelist was coming for a revival and I was excited to be there to hear him preach.

The first evening that my husband, daughter and I arrived, the pastor of our church came up to us and said to me, "This man is known for the healings that take place at his services. If he calls for anyone to come up to receive a healing, you take your daughter."

I sat there and thought about that one a while. I looked at my husband and said, "Why do we have to take her up there for a healing, when I know that God can heal her right now in this very seat?"

The evangelist began to preach and as his words went forth, I felt the Lord come down. I don't know how to explain it except to say that my daughter was playing on the pew next to me and there was a distance between her and I. I literally felt the Lord come down from Heaven and I felt His presence so strongly that I just knew in my spirit that He was sitting in between us. It was so strong that it was overwhelming. I'd never felt anything like that before. I was afraid to turn my head and look that way, because I didn't know what I was going to see. Then, just as I felt Him come, He went upwards into Heaven. I felt His presence leave.

After the service, they asked for testimonies and I said, "My daughter was just healed!" I shared what had happened. The evangelist said many times in other services, people were healed when they just heard the word of God being spoken, right in their seats. I thought this was so amazing and wonderful. I knew I felt His presence for certain. I somehow knew more than anything though that it was very important for me to voice that healing immediately, telling others and walking on that faith right away.

The next day, my daughter was scheduled for another cat scan and as she and I stood in the lobby of her doctor's office gazing out the window at the Cleveland skyline, I turned to her and said, "Honey, I really believe the Lord healed you." She said, "I know He did mom. He told me that I was going to be ok." With that being said, they called her name for the cat scan.

That doctor visit was remarkable. As we sat together waiting on the results to be told to us, the doctor just shook his head in amazement. He finally turned to me and said, "Well, this is strange, but it appears the tumor has shrunk." I was joyous! I knew it! I thanked God. He said, "This never happens and it can not be explained." I could explain it. We'd prayed for a miracle. Thank you Lord! My daughter stabilized after that for a long time, however, in a few months we would be back at the hospital again.

My marriage began to suffer great stress. I don't know if we were just so young and unable to handle the stress of a marriage as well as a very sick child or what the problem was, but I began to realize that things were not right. We fought often and I was very restless and in need of some time off. I would never let anyone baby-sit because I was afraid that she'd have a medical symptom and no one would know what to do. I trusted my mother very much with her but she was uncomfortable watching her for the same reason. I began to resent being confined at home with no outside interests. My husband resented the responsibility as well and had given up his hobbies too. It was a downward spiral.

After the years of turmoil we decided that we both really did still love each other and we planned for the birth of our second child. A son was born to us when our daughter was four years old. I can't tell you how many times I examined him, afraid that the same symptoms would appear in this child, but he was fine and born healthy. I thanked the Lord. We had somewhat of a break for a while and I felt happy again.

Around the time when our son was about two years old and our daughter was six, we were at church and I saw my daughter rub her eyes and look at the preacher and then rub her eyes again. I asked her what was wrong. She said, "Mommy, I see two of him." I was alarmed. I took her to the restroom, thinking she'd been staring too long and had somehow crossed her eyes. We washed her eyes with water and she said no, it's still there. We left early and were on our way home, when she said, "It's gone now!" and although I was relieved, I had great concern.

Early the next morning, although her eyesight was still fine, I called the neurologist at Cleveland Clinic and they scheduled her to come in immediately. On the way there, she saw the Terminal Tower in Cleveland's skyline and rubbed her eyes again and said, "There are two buildings mom." My heart sank.

The doctor examined her and turned off the light and looked into her eyes. He switched on the light and said, "I don't know how you knew to get her here in time." I said, "What?" I was thinking to myself, your child sees two of everything and who would fool around with a symptom like that. He said, "The pressure is building up behind her eyes. The fluid on the brain is increasing. I don't know how you knew to get her here. Some would have waited a bit longer. I'm glad you got her here. We have to admit her and drain the fluid off the brain. It will mean a shunt and surgery probably, but let me check with my colleagues first. Right now let me get her admitted. If you'd have waited she could have gone blind as a result of the pressure on her eyes. You did well getting her here. I want you to know that this means that the tumors have probably started to grow now." With that, he walked out of the room.

Several doctors and specialists decided that the best course of treatment was to drain the fluid off in a spinal tap and see if it could be treated in that manner, before they placed a shunt inside. They took more x-rays and concluded that the tumors had not grown. The doctor said that this now meant that we had a different medical condition on our hands now. Not even related to her tumors. He labeled this one Pseudo-tumor, which is all of the symptoms of a growing brain tumor, but there is nothing there.

It was a rough few days as they did one spinal tap after another. They had a resident doctor perform the procedure because he was more practiced at it than the neurologists were. This man's heart was wonderful and caring towards my daughter and I was grateful for that. It was difficult explaining to her what was going to happen, but I knew she'd do much better to be prepared for the procedure. She listened and accepted that this was how it had to be. The spinal tap was painful and I opted to be in the room with her. I could have fainted except that I knew if I did, they'd never allow me to stay with her again. I tried to stay focused and help hold her still and comfort her. As she cried out in pain, the doctor said, "I'm sorry sweetheart." She said, "Oh that's ok. I was just thinking of you. I'm sure it's hard on you." He looked up at me surprised that this small kindergarten age child would say that to him, and I saw tears in his eyes.

This was the first of many spinal taps. The fluid continued to build up, time and time again. Each time that it did, the double vision would return, so we knew it was high again and they'd take her in and place a gage on the needle that was inserted into her back and they would drain off the excess until it was normal levels again. I can't tell you how many times that was repeated. It was many, many times.

Around the third or fourth day that we were there, I was standing in her room, exhausted and looking at all of the flowers and cards. Her class had sent her in some wonderful cards and I realized how many people had been praying for her. My prayer to God was just please, no surgery. I told him I couldn't handle that. No. The doctor walked in and said that in all this time the fluid continued to keep building up and that we couldn't keep putting her through all of these spinal taps. They were going to try and give her steroids and if that didn't work, she would be scheduled for a shunt. They released her to my care and I was to steadily increase the steroids over the course of several days and return at any sign of headache or double vision. In a few days they would repeat the spinal tap procedure one more time.

I had to monitor her eating while on the steroids so she wouldn't gain weight. I was praying so hard for her healing and several pastor's came and laid hands upon her.

On our return visit the resident doctor who performed her procedure was not available and another doctor had to do the spinal tap. Although he had the knowledge he said it had been many years since he'd done this one. I was nervous. As he was inserting the needle into her back, he yelled, "Shoot!" I said, "What?" He said I hit a vein. I looked down to see blood everywhere and it was spurting on the sheets. I was fainting. I excused myself to go the restroom and I threw water on my face. I sunk to my knees and asked God to please guide that doctor's hand and protect my daughter and let this end. I went back into the room to find my husband bent over with his head down and I knew he was about to faint as well. He walked out when I took his place. He later told me that he too, went to the restroom and washed his face and fell to his knees asking God for help.

The spinal tap finally was in place and the gage placed there and it registered normal. We had a normal reading. Praise God. This meant the steroids worked and no shunt and no surgery. Praise the Lord. We slowly weaned her back off of the steroids and she resumed a normal life, still seizure free. The fluid did not return.

Our daughter was also weaned off of her seizure medication because she had remained seizure free for 5 years. This was a miracle. I shared our testimony with many people.

Just as I was beginning to rest and enjoy our lives, I was hit with another hard blow. We had just moved into a mobile home near my parents and we didn't have much but we had healthy and happy kids and I was glad to be close to family and friends. It was short lived though. My husband of ten years and father of my two children left me and filed for divorce. I was devastated.

I went to my parents and they showered me with love. My dad sat up with me half of one whole night, telling me that I'd be just fine. He embraced me, taking me into his arms and telling me that I'd be ok.

I loved my Dad very much. However, this thing he did for me in coming to me in my hurt and wrapping his arms around me was exactly what I needed. How often when we hurt, do we just need the arms of our Father?

I still sank into depression. I went to bed for days and my mother and father helped me with the kids. One day my dad begged me to just get up. In fact he insisted that enough was enough. I didn't want to get up. I didn't know that I'd ever love again. He sat and talked to me saying that I had to get up, that the kids needed me. This time I heard his words and that was the start of my new life.

I began to put myself through medical secretary courses. I would go at night and study in the day. I would take the children to the field near our mobile home and they would play while I studied. Soon a whole crowd of neighborhood kids would join them and I'd put my books down and make them necklaces out of clover flowers tied together.

One day a man came out of his mobile home nearby and sat in a lawn chair, placing it where he could watch the kids playing. He'd often see me making the necklaces and I'd smile at him. Mid afternoon he would leave and wave at me as he drove off.

I spoke with a friend of mine, telling her how sweet and attractive this guy seemed to be. I said I'd love to get to know him better, but how? I was too shy to approach him. I said, "Perhaps a note?"

I got out the typewriter and began to type a small note. It said, "You may not know me very well, but you've waved at me a few times when I really needed a friendly hello. As you can see, I'm a bit behind in the times, but would it be ok for a lady to ask a gentleman to dinner sometime?" I signed it with my first name and phone number.

I placed the tiny note in a small envelope. I wanted to make sure he'd know that it was the lady who sat in that field and so, I made a clover necklace. I used a hole-punch to put a hole through the corner of the envelope and threaded the necklace through it. I was quite satisfied with this approach, and placed it in his mailbox when he left the next day.

A few days later, I was sitting there in that field when he came out and walked over to me and said, "Are you Sue?" I said, "Yes." He said, "Are you the one who put the note in my mailbox?" I said, "Yes." We introduced ourselves. His name was Mark and he invited me to dinner that weekend and I, very nervously accepted.

I was still feeling very hurt over my husband walking out on me and I can't say it was the best time to start a new relationship, but it felt good to have someone so nice, treat me so nice in return.

Mark refused to take me out until he saw my divorce papers and I respected him very much for that.

I knew everyone who lived in the mobile home park and they all said Mark was known for mowing lawns for the elderly and helping out his neighbors. Even the landlord said he was a good man and I couldn't find much better.

Mark treated me with such respect and he was so pleasant to be around. As time passed and we continued to date, he often fed the children and I, because after I paid the rent there just wasn't much left.

When he began to stop by and open my refrigerator, he'd look at me and just say, "Come on, we are all going out to eat."

Christmas came and he spent so much on my children. They wouldn't have had much of a Christmas if it hadn't been for him.

Mark and I fell in love and one Christmas he asked me to marry him and I eagerly accepted. It was one of the happiest moments of my life.

Our wedding was held in a local metro park on June 20th, 1992 and it was the coldest day June 20th had seen. It broke a record. It was wet and had rained up until a few hours before the ceremony. Everyone came wearing their winter coats.

Two weeks after we were married there, in that same exact spot, a tornado came through the park and leveled the woods and many trees covered the area that we stood on to say our vows. To this day, that field that we stood on is no longer a field but now wooded. We joked that this was a sign of our lives together. It became quite a whirlwind.

CHAPTER THREE

Terror

The children and I moved into Mark's mobile home with him. It was quite an adjustment for a 34-year-old bachelor. I was 28 years old at the time.

I began to feel uncomfortable in this new place. I'd open the door at night to find that the television set was on and not on a set channel. It was a blank and rolling screen. It never seemed to come on by itself when we were home. It would only come on at night when we weren't home.

Being a newly married couple we had disagreements. I remember one night in particular we were in bed discussing something and as our voices began to grow louder, the lights in the room began to flicker on and off. When we stopped, so did the lights. This made me very uneasy. Mark would say that it was just a short in the wiring. He could easily write it off. This happened to us there several times.

One year into our marriage we purchased a home. It was an over 100 year old colonial home in a small railroad town that seemed at the time to be quaintly suspended in time. There was an upstairs, middle floor and then a basement level. We found out that home was for sale because of the fact that the man who owned it had committed suicide. He hadn't done it in the home, but in an apartment down the street.

This is how the history of the house goes. The last family who lived there owned the home for over 20 years. From what we have been told, it was a family in turmoil. We'd heard that the gentleman, who owned the home, drank excessively as well as the fact that there were other problems.

The man and woman divorced with the husband moving down the street into an apartment building and the woman staying in the home. Eventually she remarried and moved away and left the home in the care of their son and daughter.

We were told that one night after being stopped by the police for DUI, the man who owned the home, took a walk through it and then went to his apartment and got out a gun and pulled the trigger, shooting directly into his own head, committing suicide. We weren't told the full story until a few days after we'd moved in, by some of our neighbors.

There are remnants of an old well in our back yard and we were told that when the house was built there was no electricity and there was an outhouse in the backyard.

We had also been told that witchcraft and many other hideous things were performed in an old barn that once stood across the street from us.

One neighbor told us of finding satanic ritual evidence on his mothers' property right down the road. The house and town have a great deal of history.

One week after moving in, I was settling down in bed. My son was asleep in the upstairs bedroom that was next to mine. He was 6 years old and in the first grade. My daughter was 10 and she was asleep in the bedroom on the first floor that was off of our living room. My husband was working 2nd shift and didn't get home until 2:30 in the morning. We had no pets.

I felt uneasy in the house and chalked it up to the fact that it was a strange and unfamiliar place. I was reading in bed about 11:30 pm when I felt the end of the bed dip down as though someone had sat on it. I put the book down and sat up and saw no one there. This happened numerous times, night after night in that bedroom. I never saw anyone.

One weekend my husband and I went to bed together. Just as we settled into bed, the bed dipped down on my side. I sat up and said, "Did you feel that? The bed just dipped like someone sat on it." He thought I was being silly. He never felt it.

Another night about midnight, I heard my son rustling through his school papers. I wondered what he was doing at that time of the night. I yelled, "Go to sleep honey, it's not time to get up!" He didn't answer. I got up and walked into his room, which was dark. The window was closed and there were no papers anywhere to be seen.

Another night I woke up at 4:00 am to hear my daughter in her bedroom below ours on the first floor. She was going through her closet, as I could distinctly hear her coat hangers sliding back and forth in her closet. I assumed she thought it was time to get ready for school and I was giggling that she was mixed up. I went downstairs and into her room to tell her it was too early, only to find her asleep in her bed, the light off and her closet door closed. I ripped open the closet door, only to find nothing. Not even a coat hanger swinging.

Once my husband and I were asleep and we kept our bedroom door closed. There was a loud knock on our bedroom door. It was a series of 3 knocks. I yelled, "Come on in," thinking that it was one of the kids. No answer. The door didn't open. I got up and opened the door and there was no one there. This had happened several different times.

One afternoon shortly after moving in, my husband and I were grilling on the back patio. We were deep in conversation when we both saw out the corner of our eyes, a black shadow come down the back door steps. I just thought maybe a lost dog or something. We finished talking and I couldn't stop wondering what it was. I walked over to the steps and looked in front of the garage where it went. There was nothing to be seen. My husband saw the look on my face and asked me if I saw that too. I said, "Yes! Did you?" He said yes. Only later did he admit that it was the form of a human and not that of a dog, as I thought.

Many times the house would fill with smoke or a strong odor of smoke. We would have our neighbor, a firefighter, come and check it out and there would be nothing explainable about it. Our dining room filled with smoke, then it disappeared as they searched for the cause. Another time we woke up with the entire bedroom filled with smoke. I woke my husband up and as we scrambled to get out, it went away, quickly.

One night we were all asleep, and I was facing my husbands back in bed. I turned over to the open side of the bed. I saw as I turned over the black shadow of a man leaning over me. He had curly hair and was staring into my face. It was too dark for me to make out any features but I felt that he was curious about me and also glaring angrily at me. I took a quick startled intake of breath and as I did, he seemed just as startled that I saw him. He quickly backed up from me and flew backwards into the closet (which was closed) and was gone. I realized that his form got smaller as it backed away from me. I was up with the light on crying and telling my husband what I saw. He didn't believe me. He said it was a shadow probably of my own hair or something.

We often had a campfire in the back yard and our neighbors

would join us around the fire and we had some good conversations out there. On this one particular night, I had put my son to bed and he came outside much later in his pajamas, to the fire. He said, with tears in his eyes, "Mom… something bad is going to happen." I said, "Oh no, no, no sweetie. Everyone and everything is fine." Everyone asked what was wrong and I told all of them what he had said. Mark came over and said, "No, you don't worry now, we are all fine." I took my son and tucked him back into bed, but you could see the stress and worry on his face. I couldn't stop thinking about the time when I was a child and I knew that something bad was going to happen and my family was involved in that car accident. He had me concerned. He couldn't tell me much more. He just kept saying, "I don't know what but something bad is going to happen."

Within one week of that evening my husband Mark was involved in a very serious car accident. He took his eyes off of the road and when he looked back up, he saw a dump truck stopped right in front of him. He hit it while traveling 50 mph and did not have his seat belt on that day. He always wore his seatbelt. He does not know why that one particular day it was forgotten.

I received the phone call that afternoon and I was hysterical and the nurse had me speak to him so that I would know that he was ok and I could hear his voice. He said hello to me, but his speech was very slurred. I was frightened.

I entered the emergency room to find him in bad shape. He had broken his sternum bone in his chest and there was nothing they could do for that. His heart had been in arrhythmia but had stabilized. He had gone into the windshield of his pickup truck and his head cracked the windshield. Half of his eyebrow was missing and still pinched in the glass where the glass had expanded and contracted upon cracking. He had a large cut where his chin hit the dash. From the force of the accident and his head going forward, it threw his tongue forward and he in turn, bit down on it, cutting into it more than half way. This was why his speech was so slurred. His tongue was gouged and a mess.

They admitted him for overnight observation and the next morning he had to be put into surgery to repair his tongue. It was a painful surgery that he had to be awake for and with the broken sternum he couldn't sit down or get up without help. It was weeks of recovery.

A woman who lived in town and who also worked with him came to visit him after he arrived home from the hospital. She stopped in our doorway, and said, "This is where you live? Do you know the turmoil that went on in this house?" She refused to stay and visit. She said she couldn't breathe here. She said she knew the people who lived in the house prior and she said, "I can't believe this is where you live. I can't stay here!" She immediately left.

Another hard blow came when my daughter Rachel came home from school and while folding laundry went into a seizure. The seizures had returned. We rushed her off to the emergency room to get her stabilized and they placed her back on seizure medications after years of total healing. A pastor of a local church called me and said that he'd received the news and wondered if we needed prayer. I told him that I always welcomed prayer. I said, "But I know that its just satan trying to make me doubt that she was healed way back then." I told him that we had faith that God would see her through. He'd healed her and I was standing on that. He said he was amazed at my words. Rachel, being back on seizure medication, finally stabilized again and returned to school.

There were other problems surfacing within Rachel though. She seemed to uncontrollably lie to us over little things and she was uncontrollably eating. She would purposely go against us and we continued to receive many shocking reports from school about her behavior. These situations added to the stress in our household. It seemed she constantly needed to be watched, because we didn't know what to expect next.

My son came to me one morning. He was about 10 years old now. He began to tell me that something had pulled the blankets off of him last night. I said, "No, it was probably the cat." He said no, that the cat was shut up in the basement. He had just gone to bed and was pulling his blankets up around his face when they were being tugged away from him. He looked down at the floor and could see the blankets being pulled. He said that he could see the finger marks in the material, where the fingers should have been, but weren't. He told us that he had tried to call me and was so scared that the word, 'Mom', would not come out. My son didn't sleep all night. I still tried to rationalize it away. I said it was probably a dream. He said, "No, mom".

One night, many nights after my son's story of the blankets, I got up out of my bed to go the downstairs restroom. After a drink of water I hurried back to bed. I had just gotten into bed and was pulling the blankets up around me and I turned my back to my husbands' back, to settle into sleep. Instantly the blankets were yanked off of us and pulled under the bed. It was a hard, "human like" tug. Not one that a cat could do. My husband stirred in his sleep and tried to pull the blankets back and they were still being tugged, as I watched unable to move. He turned over and looked at me when immediately the blankets were released and he said, "What are you doing?" I said, "I didn't do that".

I demanded that he get up and turn the light on and look under that bed. The cat wasn't in our room or under the bed. Our bedroom door was closed. There was nothing under our bed. It was just as my son had explained.

After that incident I began to be terrified in my own home. When my husband worked nights, I sat up in the living room until he got home in the early hours of morning. He used to ask me why I couldn't just go to sleep. When we went to bed I made him hold me. I never allowed him to turn his back to me for long, because I'd cry and beg for him to put his arms around me again. This created a great deal of stress in our household. The only way I slept was when he was in the bed with me, holding me, and I was reciting the

Lords prayer in my mind over and over again. I felt very much comforted by the part, "deliver us from evil."

My husband Mark and I soon had a child of our own. A beautiful little girl, who was born with the worst case of colic I'd ever seen or heard about. She seemed to cry constantly and only I could hold her. Sometimes my husband would hold her so I could get some sleep. She rarely let anyone, even grandparents, hold her. She seemed to immediately know the change of the faces and even over time, never seemed to recognize them, as a baby. The grandparents would come over and pass her back to me saying, "I don't know how to help you."

During that time I rocked in the rocking chair so much that my head would spin when I was out of it. It was a very stressful time. She often seemed terrorized or frightened and would scream out suddenly as though in pain. That scream in the middle of the night would send both of our hearts racing in fear of what was wrong. It was very hard on us all.

The doctors told me that it happens to some children who are born more alert and aware of their surroundings. He said that it should pass by the time she was a month old, and then he said well, maybe two months old, and as this continued on and on, he said he'd never seen a case last so long.

We had placed her crib in our bedroom with us. Often her pacifiers would come up missing. I just assumed they'd fallen in to the couch or something similar. I was constantly purchasing pacifiers.

One day I'd had enough, and tipped the couch over and vacuumed in it and under it, looking for a spare. Not one pacifier was found. I then began to wonder what was happening to them.

One night we were down to one pacifier that was left. I prayed that this one didn't come up missing. In the middle of the night our daughter screamed suddenly and I switched on the light. There was no pacifier to be found. I removed all of her blankets and there was no pacifier. My husband got up and we even took her mattress out of her crib and turned it over and looked under the bed. Nothing. The bedroom had been recently newly carpeted and was not cluttered in any way. There was just no pacifier in that room. I was so frustrated and went downstairs to search in a kitchen drawer for one.

Several of our friends enjoyed hearing the ghost stories, and I have to admit that in the daytime I enjoyed telling them. They had suggested that I talk to this ghost and ask it what it wanted. I didn't want to acknowledge it. I didn't want to speak to it. I was afraid it would make it worse.

Well, that night, I stopped and looked up and yelled loudly.... "OK! I've had enough! Put it back!", to whatever unseen force was in our home. My husband called down to me in a strange voice, "Sue, come here!" I walked upstairs thinking, no way. He had it in his hand and looked at me strangely and said when he heard me say that, he turned around and there it was, right in the middle of the floor, where moments before we had just checked.

One of the strangest incidents that we have experienced was when the phone rang in the middle of the night. My husband ran downstairs to answer it thinking something was wrong with a family member for the phone to be ringing that time of the night. I sat up in bed listening to his conversation on the phone at the bottom of the stairs. The house was very quiet and I could hear the woman's voice on the other end of the phone. Mark said, "No, I'm sorry, she's in the bed already. Can I take a message?" I heard a woman screaming on the other end, all the way up the stairs. Mark remained quiet and then I heard him quietly put the phone back on the base. He slowly walked up the steps and sat on the end of our bed, scratching his head. I said, "Who was that? What did she want?" He said it was the strangest thing. The woman on the other end of the phone knew his name and my name and asked for me. She called us by name. When he told her I was in bed, the woman lost it and went hysterically insane. She began hatefully screaming at him that it was her house and she would come over here if she had to. She said I was her daughter. He said it was a horrible and evil voice. Unlike any he'd ever heard before.

We tried to think it was a wrong number. Perhaps it was just an intoxicated woman who had called the wrong place. Yet, how did this woman know our names? How strange that it frightened us the way that it did. I began to wonder if it was a call from the other side.

One Saturday afternoon, I was in the bathroom on the first floor and I heard the back door open and someone come inside. I heard the footsteps going to the base of our stairs. I then heard a girl call up the stairs, "Rachel, are you up there?" Rachel is my oldest daughter that had the brain tumor. I heard no response from my daughter but I knew she was upstairs. I couldn't figure out why she wouldn't answer her friend. Finally I heard the person walk up the stairs. I heard our very old stairs creak with each step. It was always easy to know when someone was walking up the steps.

I finished up and went outside and found my husband sitting on the back steps of the door that had just opened to our guest. I asked him who had come over to visit with Rachel. He said no one. He said he was sitting there the whole time. I told him that I had heard the door open and finished telling him the story of hearing the young girl call to Rachel and go up the stairs. We walked inside and I called up to Rachel who responded. I said, "Who is up there with you?" She said, "No one." I walked up to her room and there was no one there. When I told her the story she looked as scared and shocked as I was.

I'd try to ask my husband after each incident, "Do you believe me now?" He would just say that if we had a ghost why didn't he see as much as I did?

One evening while laying in bed reading, my husband and I had an argument. He stormed out of the room and I went back to reading my book. I heard his footsteps bounding the stairs angrily. Then I heard him throw a book up the stairs! I could hear the pages twirling in the wind as it flew up the steps and hit the wall at the landing on top. I couldn't believe him doing something like that! He came angrily back up the steps and stepped into our bedroom. He stood there with his hands on his hips. He looked at me and yelled, "How dare you throw that book!" I said, "I didn't throw the book!" I showed him it was still in my hand. He just looked at me puzzled. I said I'd thought that he threw the book. We got up and looked and there was no book on the stairs. No book to be found.

When our daughter was about 2 years old, we combined the two girls bedrooms. We put my oldest daughter in the bedroom that used to be my husbands and mine, along with the youngest. The two girls could share that room and my husband and I took the basement and turned that in to our bedroom. We had a baby monitor so we could always hear our children upstairs.

My oldest daughter began to report the same knocks on her door in the middle of the night that I had heard. She also had an angel on her headboard and every morning that she woke up, the angel would be turned around to face the wall. One of her music boxes would go off unexplainably in the middle of the night.

Cassidy's toy box was in the living room and many nights my husband would get up because her toys had begun to play by themselves. Music would start or dolls would begin singing and talking, as though someone were playing with them. I'd again ask my husband, "Do you believe me NOW?" He would say, "Oh this is so ridiculous, the toys just settled and set each other off."

I went to a local ladies meeting, in our hometown and there was a guest speaker. I recognized him as someone I knew from school. He claimed to be psychic and paranormal expert. He showed us a slide presentation of photograph after photograph of "ghosts" that he supposedly had captured on film. I was drawn immediately into this. After the meeting ended, I asked him if he could come into our home and perhaps tell me what he felt was there. He readily agreed. (Please let me tell you right now, if you are having problems in your home and are considering inviting someone like this to come over and investigate, don't do it. It opened the door to even more demonic activity. Do not seek help from anyone other than Christians, trained in deliverance.)

This man came into our home one evening at 11:00 pm at night. He told us that it was the best time to catch them on film. (Isn't that just like evil? It prefers darkness, doesn't it?)

The man took out a pendulum hanging from a chain and began to hold it in various places around the house. It began to twirl uncontrollably about and at that precise moment, he took a picture. He said he had to make sure that the energy had built enough to catch them on film. He shared that he could examine anyone's photographs by holding the pendulum over them and if it truly were a real ghost, it would cause the pendulum to swing. (Evil works in that way, even through photographs.)

Next, he brought out divining rods. These he carried around the house and explained that they would cross each other and move back and forth at the area of increased energy. (I didn't know it at the time, but I was allowing satanic rituals and satanic tools to be brought into our home.)

After wandering about the house and taking many photos he sat down to talk with us and give us his analogy.

He felt it was an older gentleman haunting our home, that had died of lung disease and that this older gentleman was attached to my son and liked him. He also added that he felt that many people came in the past to check on him and that was why we were hearing the knocks on our doors. They were, according to him, repeated patterns of the past. Energy, he claimed, that was being replayed. (This man was a deceived man himself. He was spending most of his free time seeking the dark evil side. He was using pagan tools with which to do this with. He shared with me that these "presences" often followed him home at night and would pick on him. He didn't know how much he was opening the door and giving them free reign to his life.)

We didn't find much comfort from that man's visit. (In fact, things began to worsen quickly in our home.) We knew one thing, that the knocks on our door weren't replayed energy. They were from a definite presence.

I received an email of a photograph from that man a few days later, that he had taken in our home while visiting. This photograph had a circular path of light circling over Rachel's bed. He said, "There is your ghost!" We didn't sleep any better.

When our little one was 4 years old, she was playing outside in the back yard one morning. She came in and said, "Rachel where are you?" She was laughing as though she was in the middle of a game with Rachel. I said, "Honey, Rachel isn't here. What do you need?" She said, "Then who is calling me? Yes, she's here! I just heard her calling my name! She was playing a game with me." I said, "No, sweetie, she isn't. She isn't here."

She sat down on the kitchen floor and began to cry. I picked her up and said that it was going to be ok. She said that someone was calling her name and playing hide and go seek with her. I went outside, thinking it was just one of the neighbors' children playing with her, and no one was home. Not even one neighbor around anywhere.

One evening as I was tucking her into bed she looked at me strangely. She said, "Mommy when you check on me tonight, will you wear the same nightgown that you wore last night?" I said, "Which nightgown? What color was it?" She said it was one she'd never seen before. She described it to me and it was nothing like anything I owned.

Another night afterward, she said to me, "Was that you in my room last night?" I said, "Why sweets, what did you see?" She said she saw a woman that was kind of like me but not me, standing in front of her TV and pointing to the TV with a gun in her hand. She went on to describe in detail the color of the gun and the description of the handle.

I was frightened. I still tried to assume it must have been a dream. However if these so called ghosts were going to appear with weapons in their hands in front of my children, I had to do something. Then my oldest daughter had a story to tell.

One morning my little one woke up screaming and terrified. It was 5 am and I went up to check on her and she was shaking and asking me to put her on the couch downstairs, "Right now", she said. I picked her up, turning off the bedroom light as I left the room. Soon we feel back asleep on the couch.

When my oldest daughter came downstairs later that morning she said, "Mom I saw her!" She said, "You know how you turned off the light when you left our room? I went back to sleep for a while and then I woke up and turned over. There she was."

She said she was standing in the middle of the room and looking from her bed to my youngest daughters bed, almost as though she was wondering where the little one went. She said it was then just staring at her.

My daughter said, "Mom she looks like you!" She described her. She was wearing an old-fashioned nightgown with lacey cuffs and having features a lot like me, only she described her as having longer hair that was turned under. When Rachel became frightened and gasped, the woman disappeared and faded.

Through out the years in our home we were unable to keep brand new appliances in the home. In 8 years we had been through at least 6 or more phones, two computers, two dishwashers, two dryers, two furnaces, two hot water tanks. The stove and refrigerator both broke

Terror

at the same time once.

The refrigerator would dump water in the floor and it would only happen in the middle of the night. I would wake up and there would be a large puddle on the floor.

Once while I was talking on the phone, I was shocked in my ear as the phone began to crackle and sizzle as though burning up. Our phones would often ring and we'd pick them up and no one would be there.

Our home was struck by lightening twice, the first time it hit our brand new furnace and the second time it ruined our new computer.

This was just too much to comprehend. It began to create such enormous stress between us. Many times I didn't know why we stayed there, or how our marriage survived those years.

One evening, I decided to take my husbands pick-up truck and drive to the store. It was dark outside and I walked out of the house and unlocked the truck and got inside. I put the key in the ignition and just as I was about to start the truck, it began to shake. The truck was rocking from side to side. I thought a neighbor was playing a prank on me and I looked behind me in the rear view mirror and could see nothing. It seemed to be coming from the bed of the truck, as if someone was inside it and purposely shaking it to frighten me. I reached over and locked the doors. Just when I was about to hit the horn to get some help, the shaking stopped. I felt a rattling as though someone was walking across the bed of the truck and then I heard someone jump down. The whole time, I was looking back there and could not see a figure at all. I ran in the house and told Mark and again he shrugged it off.

I had not slept well at night and we had been there for 8 years now. My husband was very skeptical and I couldn't get him to discuss it very much. I didn't know what the black shadow was that we saw. I didn't know whom the man was that I saw. I didn't know what the woman was that my daughters have seen.

Was it the activity of the last family and the man who killed himself? Or was it someone from way back, since the house is over 100 years old. I didn't know.

Things didn't happen as often as before, but we always knew we were not alone in that house. I would constantly recite The Lords Prayer silently at night before bed and ask that He keep us from evil.

When I had finally begun to relax a bit, we had another major problem arise. The CO detector began to go off intermittently during the day. Mark came home and it was still going off and he had me to call our neighbor, the fire fighter who came out with some men from the fire department.

They found the levels of carbon monoxide to be dangerously high in our basement. The rest of the house tested normal. It seemed to be a ventilation problem with our hot water tank. They shut if off and advised us to clean out the vent, as it was probably a bird's nest.

The next day, when the vent was taken apart and checked it was totally clear of any debris. There was no explanation for why, after 8 years, this hot water tank had stopped venting.

Our neighbors helped and along with Mark they raised the vent higher, to a larger peak of our house. It still was not venting. Carbon Monoxide would still seep into the basement. We were puzzled and worried.

Within a few days of us wondering what step to take next, the vent on the hot water tank suddenly began to work, just as though we'd never had a problem. It has never given us a problem venting, since.

After the Sept. 11th tragedy that hit our country, I had a prophetic dream. My mother in law, Margo, called me all night, through this dream, telling me, "We will not have a spirit of fear! God does not want us to live in fear!" She begged me to tell her son the message. I agreed. But in the dream I got busy and she kept calling, saying to tell him that we will not live in fear. She wouldn't give up until I told him. When I told him, in my dream, what his mother's message was, I woke up instantly.

After sharing the dream with Mark that morning, I called Margo, and she said, "We have been praying on this! It is my words as I pray at church and I always call out prayer for each of my family members!" We didn't know what her dream meant, but we attributed it to the discomfort and fear that America felt after that tragedy.

Cassidy began to develop night terrors and refused to play in her room upstairs. She came screaming and running down the stairs to me one afternoon, early in November 2001. I caught her in my arms and asked what was wrong. She was 5 at the time. She said there is something up there and it feels like it's about to grab me. I'd had enough. I settled her on the couch to watch TV and I went upstairs and said, "Leave my children alone!" I felt its presence so strongly that I grabbed my camera and went back up there. I thought, 'Show yourself so I can deal with you!!"

I snapped a photo in the direction of that room from the hallway. When I examined the photo, I was able to see three faces in the glass of a curio cabinet that was in that room. Not everyone has been able to see what I see, but many pick out the faces right away. Identified by a neighbor, was the face of the man who lived here before us and committed suicide. The others that we've seen in the photo are awful. One looks skeletal. The other looks mean and evil.

Now I began to know what I was dealing with. This wasn't a silly ghost story. This wasn't a friendly resistant ghost. This wasn't a person, who didn't pass on to the light. They were there. Evil beings were in my home and I knew it.

Next, Cassidy began to complain that something sat on her bed at night and moved her blankets. Then she mysteriously fell ill. She would wake up and vomit, only at 4 am, about once a week. The first week of November 2001, she woke up on a Wed. at 4 am vomiting. She was fine at daybreak, and around 8 am she even asked for breakfast.

Then the illness hit her again on Wed. in the 2nd week of November at 4 am. Once again she was on our couch very ill and then as the sun rose, she was up and playing and asking for food.

I took her to the pediatrician who said she had no logical explanation for it. She said, "Why a Wed?" I said, "I don't know." She replied, "This is strange!" The pediatrician asked if we always ate out on Tuesdays or if there was a special day at school where she ate something different. I said, "No, we rarely eat out and no, she doesn't have a snack in school. She goes to half day kindergarten and has lunch at home." There was no explanation she could give me, except to watch her and return should it begin to become more frequent. Cassidy checked out as a healthy girl.

Then the week of Thanksgiving came. Cassidy woke up on Tuesday of that week and vomited once again at 4 am. She was again fine at daybreak as the sun rose. I kept telling my husband that it was so strange and worried me greatly. We checked the CO detector. Nothing. It was fine.

On one weekend, during this same time, Mark was looking forward to watching a race on TV. I had some shopping to do and our little girl was in the bed sleeping, after being ill on this particular day, with a fever. I asked him to watch her closely.

I left and he was alone in the house with our sleeping daughter. I came home and he was yelling very loud at the race on TV and shouting for someone to win. I kept asking him to be quiet so our daughter could sleep. He'd yell, "Ok!" and then go back to his race, only to get louder.

A few hours later I asked him what was wrong? He said, "nothing!" I said, "Mark, have you been drinking?" He said, "NO!"

I noticed his speech was slurred and told him so. He walked right over to me and looked at me and began to speak and his speech was fine. I didn't know what to think of it.

I asked him to go downstairs with me. I demanded that he tell me what was wrong. He said once again, nothing.

Then I said, "Mark, tell me the truth or I will call an ambulance, because your speech is slurred and you need to be honest with me."

He said, "Why, so you can get mad at me?" I demanded again that he tell me.

"I had a couple of shots of whiskey!" He shouted.

I said, "You don't drink whiskey! You never have! Where is it?"

Mark took me in the canning room in the basement. He pointed to a shelf. I went in there and pulled out the hidden bottle of whiskey and it was 3/4ths gone. He had drunk all of that during the time I was out shopping. He was supposed to be watching Cassidy. I was so angry. I couldn't believe it. I couldn't believe that this was another situation in our lives, in my life, in our home. I couldn't believe that I was married to an alcoholic. I cried.

I smashed the bottle on the floor of our basement. I was so angry. I was about to turn around and shout that I was leaving him. I turned around and I saw something else.

He was pitiful and ashamed and confused. His head was down. I saw him, Mark, my husband, standing there somehow beneath this shell of ugly sin that wasn't him and yet was trying to become a part of him. I instantly saw Mark and something that wasn't Mark. It wasn't him, but yet it was. I found that I couldn't yell.

I said, "I love you. We love you. How could you do this?"

I didn't know what happened, but I knew that whatever possessed him, wanted me to be angry and leave. I knew this evil couldn't stand to hear that I loved my husband. He began, with slurred speech, to beg for my forgiveness.

I stayed, not sure of our future. He refused to talk to me very much about this problem. We'd have times when we were alone that I'd beg him to get some help. He'd say he'd handle it on his own.

Then he drank again within a few days and I knew it. I said this time, calmly though, that I guess we needed to separate for a while.

Mark begged me not to go. Saying he wanted his family more and to give him time. I agreed to stay once more, but knew I'd not do it a third time, if it happened again.

His drinking and our daughter Cassidy's mysterious illness all surfaced together within a few weeks of Thanksgiving. I felt at the end of my rope. Defeated and nowhere to turn. My parents knew of the problem and began to pray for us. I called my sister asking for her and her husband to get into prayer.

CHAPTER FOUR

I Will Lift Up Mine Eyes Unto The Hills From Whence Cometh My Help

Thanksgiving came and my husband's family came over to visit. His brother, Stefan, began to tell us of how he and his wife Michelle went to visit my sister in law, Lisa and her family in California.

Stefan and Michelle then shared the story of how our nephew, Lisa's son, had not been able to sleep in his bedroom at night and how he'd complain that a chair in his room was going up and down.

Stefan, Michelle and Marks mother, Margo, had been taking classes on the forces of good and evil in the world at their church, Living Water Christian Fellowship. They were studying on how to cast out demons.

They knew Lisa and her family needed help. They shared how some toys could actually contain evil curses and spirits. They talked to her about how demonic presences could be in our homes and lives.

The whole time that they were visiting, our nephew kept asking for a certain toy. He kept saying over and over again, "Where is my dragon?"

No one could find this dragon that they began to feel had evil associated with it. Then, through prayer, God revealed to them that the dragon was under the couch and they found it and prayed over it and bound up the spirits associated with it. They threw it in the trash. Since that time, they shared that our nephew sleeps so much better.

I couldn't contain myself. I instantly began to tell them of the problems we were having in our house and about Mark's worsening drinking problem and Cassidy's strange illness.

They didn't hesitate and said that they could help us. They told me the importance that Mark would have to want the help too and to call them when we had talked and were ready.

They walked upstairs and felt the presence up there and they knew that it wasn't good. It didn't like them and Stefan said that it tried to take his breath away. It was very difficult for him to breath up there. I'd experienced the same feeling there many times.

They left our home concerned, saying to call them soon.

We once again witnessed the illness hit our daughter, Cassidy, on the Saturday after Thanksgiving at 4 am. Mark was home on this day, to witness it.

Cassie was very ill with dark circles under her eyes and a very pale complexion. It was happening more that just once a week now.

I said, to my husband Mark, "Watch her for awhile." Just as I'd predicted, as the sun rose, she began to play and ask for food. He couldn't believe it and couldn't understand it. We were both so worried.

I pulled him aside. I said, "You have to listen to me. We have a demon in our house. It has been here since we moved in. It is getting worse."

I said, "Your brother said it is important for you to believe me first, so we can get rid of it. He says he knows how to get it out of here."

I reminded Mark of his worsening drinking and how out of control it had become and how the man who lived here before did the same and committed suicide. I asked him if he felt there could be a connection.

I reminded him of the evil forces we had seen, the phone call we had gotten, and the smoke in the house.

Then I said that I believed it was a demonic presence that was seeking to destroy him and our marriage. I said, but more importantly, I believed it was after our daughter with this illness. I told him it was out to destroy our family.

I waited anxiously praying inside that he'd hear my words. He said, "I'm with you on this. Let's call them."

I called his mom the next morning and she said that they would arrive at our home that evening.

My two older children weren't home that night when they all arrived and we had arranged previously for the neighbor to keep Cassidy.

Margo, Stefan, Michelle, Mark and I, gathered in our living room. We anointed our hands with oil, prayed together and prayed for deliverance and the binding of the evil that was there, and then we went upstairs to pray.

We gathered in a circle together in that upstairs bedroom and held hands, praying. The floor then began to shake under our feet. Michelle described it later as a stomping of feet in anger. I heard and felt it more as a rumble, as though a kitchen chair was being bounced around in our circle.

I began to feel that I couldn't breathe. It was taking my breath away. I felt such fear and I wanted to run. I, who had been in prayer for months, couldn't stand to hear the prayer that they were saying any longer, because as they prayed I was getting worse. I was going to faint.

I ran out of the room and I stood at the door and I shouted, "I can't do this!"

Michelle came and grabbed my hands and she said, "Oh no, no! You WILL stay here. Spirit of Fear, I bind you in the Name of Jesus Christ! You leave her alone."

She held her hands up and said, "Sue, put your hands right here on mine." I did.

She said, "Say it Sue! Say, 'Leave me alone you spirit of fear.'"

(The prophetic dream I'd had, of my mother in law, Margo, telling me that we will not live in fear, was now very much making sense to me.)

She said, "Say it!" I couldn't speak it. My words came out jumbled, held back and choked out like a whisper.

She kept on repeating it and saying, "Say it Sue!"

I struggled to say it and closing my eyes, finally got the words out and immediately, it left me. I felt this evil spirit of fear, lift off of me as though someone lifted a blanket off of my head.

I opened my eyes and looked up and Stefan was staring at me with this smile on his face. I said, "Should we pray some more now?" And he said, "Praise God! We sure should!"

Mark was staring at me shocked at what he'd witnessed. He said you could see fear and terror spread across my face and then leave.

We went back into praying. Michelle's face was very red and her neck was red and she was shaking. It appeared as though she'd fought a major battle and won, I thought to myself.

We kept praying and calling the spirits out by name, any spirits that came to mind. They called out the mans name (the man who previously owned the home) and said, "You familiar spirit connected to this man, you will have no connection to this house... you will exist here no more... you are bound up and all communications are broken."

The bed, Cassidy's bed, began to shift and move as though

being pushed! There was this agonizing push on the bed as though this spirit was in torment, as we prayed. I knew it didn't like what was being done. It didn't matter to me. Fear was off of me and I wanted it out now.

Next we anointed our hands once more, asking God to bless us and we walked around the room and prayed over the beds, the closet, the walls, and the floor, commanding anything evil to leave and asking God's Holy Spirit to come in.

I felt that it was clean now, and that we'd succeeded, except for this one corner, so I went to the corner and prayed there. Everyone began to go downstairs and I was alone in that room and I began to feel a twinge of worry.

Somehow I knew that it had come down to me. I had opened the door and unknowingly allowed these things into my home. I knew it was important that I face that worry and command for them to leave us alone. I did that and had such peace.

Next we all made a prayer cloth out of a small cloth and prayed God's protection, anointing and blessing upon it. We placed it under Cassidy's mattress.

They said, "Is that all?" I said "No I have to pray for Mark." So we laid hands on Mark.

I prayed for him to take the responsibility of being spiritual head of the household. I prayed that the spirits that were consuming him would now leave him alone. He kept saying "Amen. Amen." I saw that he was healed of alcoholism at that very same moment, in front of my eyes. Somehow I just knew it was gone.

My husband went to the neighbor's house to get Cassidy. She came in the door and said my tummy hurts. I held her in my lap and said lets just pray to Jesus. She began to wiggle in my arms and cover her ears and say "no, no, no, no, no!"

Michelle and I prayed softly and quietly and Cassie began to scream. "NO, NO, NO! Stop it!" We didn't give up. I looked at Michelle and we knew that a spirit had some unseen hold on Cassie. As we prayed, and she fell forward in my arms and screamed, "I am so mean! No one likes me! I am so mean!"

We immediately said, "No you are not! You are sweet and beautiful and we love you and God loves you!" We kept praying and telling her how beautiful and pretty she was and how God loves her. She began to relax and then giggle and laugh. She fell back in our arms laughing. I believe whole-heartedly that this evil was directly attacking her.

Later Mark said that he finally believed me about what all I'd seen here. He felt the floor shake. More importantly, he felt the peace afterward, like he'd never felt there before, after these demonic presences had left.

Margo said it was important that he see all of this. That was a big key to our deliverance of this terror.

On Sunday afternoon, the very next day, Margo came back with her pastors Terry and Bobby Grapenthin along with Stefan and Michelle.

We began to pray as a group and just ask for forgiveness of all sins that might have been committed there on our land, by us or anyone else. As the names came to us, we called out the demons by name... spirit of death and destruction... spirit of suicide... spirit of alcoholism... spirit of depression and oppression... spirit of poverty... spirit of loneliness and despair... spirit of sexual perversion.... spirit of anger and malice... etc. We called them out and bound them up and cut off all communications with them and sent them to dry uninhabited places, in the name of Jesus. We used our authority in Jesus to make it clear that we were taking back this land for Jesus Christ and making it God's land.

We took Communion and with Communion, we cleansed the land. This blew all religious theories out of my mind. They told us we were going to pour Jesus' blood on the ground, represented by the grape juice. I was worried about that, because of what I'd been taught. When I shared that, Pastor Terry stopped to listen to my concerns and he explained that Communion had many uses that were kept hidden by religious spirits, that didn't want us to know the power of it.

Terry prayed over the communion bread & grape juice and he said we are going to go outside, and shared that we were going to dig up the ground just a little bit at all four corners of our land.

Terry said that he sensed a spirit of witchcraft and said he felt that someone might have buried something in our land a long time ago, such as a cursed object or a blood sacrifice to satan.

He instructed Mark to dig up a piece of the land at each corner. Then he said, "I will anoint the hole with oil then you are going to pour the blood of Jesus on the land."

I said once again, "Wait. I have a problem with this. This is precious to me. The communion. I don't want to pour it on the ground." They told us that in the Old Testament people blessed their land. They wouldn't put sheep or cattle or anything on land until it was blessed. He said satan has made it so churches do not understand that this is a powerful tool of God. He said it would wash the land and claim it back as God's. It is called Redeeming the Land.

We agreed. First the oil, then the grape juice, then the bread and said, "Thank you Jesus."

Bobby, looked at me and said, "Isn't this neat? I love it!" I had a feeling of great relief sweep over me.

After the third hole was finished, we went to the last and fourth corner. As that was finished, I felt the full release and disappearance of the evil. The wind began to whip up, very mysteriously, at that fourth corner. I knew that I could feel the significance now of what we had done. This was important and good to have done.

Marks family and Terry and Bobby Grapenthin, helped us with such love and caring. We were so grateful for the acceptance and belief in our story, the instruction that they were willing and prepared to give, the truth that they didn't hesitate to share with us, and then the guidance and prayer for us and our family, and last but not least the faith that what is done in the name of Jesus, sets many free... all of this, along with our strong desire to be rid of this torment and terror... this all worked to set us free.

We came back inside our home and Bobby prophesied over Mark and I and through her, God said that we would become a tool and do this for other people and their land. That soon many would seek us out and ask for help. People that we don't even know. God's word was that we now have this gift of knowledge and have learned how to use it, and that we will go on and do this for others. That it is God's will.

Bobby was the first to tell me that I had a gift of discerning spirits because I've seen them and sensed them. I said, "I see things but I don't want to see them." She said a class that the church offers, could teach me to use that in a better way.

We began to pray and then Bobby said; "Now I have to go to your daughter." Rachel was instantly in tears. She said to Rachel, in prophesy, "You are so precious. You are beautiful. So-called friends that you have tried to please have hurt you. These friends wouldn't accept you unless you acted like them. I will make you radiant with beauty, says the Lord. You are my child. You will outshine them. If you would just turn to me... all I ask is that you turn to me and see what is in store for you. I will place upon you the gift of healing. You will look at someone and say 'oh you have a headache' and they will say how did you know. And you will lay your hands on them and they will be healed, that and greater things. Thus said the Lord," she said.

They were supposed to have a class at their church at 6:30 pm and they didn't leave here until 6:45. They said it was important and that all the steps had to be followed.

Sunday night after everyone left, we then began to throw things out. We threw out the Grimm's fairy tales. We threw out an alien picture on my son's wall. Books that we didn't feel God would want in our home. Many things we looked at differently and wanted to clean our house up for the Lord.

One of the things the pastor's took time to speak to us on was how in other countries, as well as the United States, there are people who practice witchcraft and voodoo. In the United States, we push topics that make us uncomfortable, aside. However, in other countries they know about curses and witchcraft and whether we want to believe it or not, these people who practice these pagan religions know how to use these curses as well. Many items available for purchase can have a curse placed upon it. They said you may be given a plant as a gift, or some other item, and every time you walk past it, it bothers you. Or perhaps you purchased this item and it makes you uncomfortable. We learned to pray over the object and to bind any evil associated with it in the name of Jesus and then to either burn it, break it and or throw it out. They taught us how we can unknowingly open doors and give legal right for Satan to come into our homes with these things.

Terry and Bobby raise Siamese kittens and one litter had just been born and they kept them at night in a bathroom where they couldn't get out. One night Terry said that he woke up and sat straight up and looked at the foot of his bed. There was a little thing that looked like a kitten sitting there. As he got up, he heard it hit the floor. He thought how did the kittens get out? Terry opened the bathroom door and looked and counted and they were all there. That same night at a separate time, his wife, Bobby woke up and saw a dark cloaked hooded figure standing by her side of the bed. The next morning she said, "Honey, death was here last night and I had to bind it up and cast it out." He said, "I saw a cat on our bed." They prayed. Bobby said she kept hearing in her spirit, "Pokeman. Pokeman." She thought, "What kind of a word is that?" She didn't know about the toy back then. Bobby asked her daughter, "Do you know anything about this word?" She said, "Yeah, it's a toy and a friend of mine gave me a key chain of it." She went and got it. They said, "Pray about it and ask God if you should get rid of it and if He says you should then you should." She said, "I will". She came to them later and said God had told her to get rid of it and that she'd thrown it away. Well the next night the same apparition appeared to Bobby. She went to her daughter again and said, "What did you do with that key chain?" She said, "It's right there in the trash can." They said "WHAT? Get it out of the house!" They researched it and found out that pokeman means pocket monster and the one she was given was Peek-a-choo and that one was the spirit of death.

My husband said, "Why isn't this stuff taught more, or on the news! Why don't churches tell us about these things?" They said we know. We know.

I began to get tears in my eyes. I said this is so sad. I said, "Do you know the number of churches I've sat in? Where they are just sitting?"

They told us to cover ourselves in the blood of Jesus before we leave in the mornings, before we run errands or go to work, or begin our day, because we may never know the people we run into, and the things we get and whether or not they are of the enemy.

They told us that it is people who have the understanding that we had just acquired, that will be used greatly by God in the end times.

God said to me one Sunday morning as I prayed, that when you see these people go to psychics or those who say they can talk to the dead, that is the dead seeking the dead. If they believed in God, they would already know there is life after death. These people aren't speaking with your relatives that have died and gone on. So many are misled by the fact that some of these psychics can call up a memory that only they and the loved one they are trying to reach would know. They are getting the information. No doubt about it. However, they aren't speaking to your loved one. They are speaking to familiar spirits and demons that already had prior knowledge of your life, because they are generational and passed on and know each of your family members and they've been around you and your loved ones, unfortunately, to know these things. I then quickly realized that I'd been seeking the dead in wondering who my ghosts were, instead of the Living God!

We lived with a demonic presence all of those years. This was a powerful demonic presence that was out to destroy us. If you have this in your home, whether it is bigger than what we've told you here, or a small detail of maybe seeing something for a moment, get it out of your house, through God's authority that we have told you about here.

I can't tell you enough how sad it makes me that many of the people we knew that are Christians, did not know the answers that were needed to help set us free. Christians, it is time to step fully into your calling in Christ Jesus. There is a dark side that we don't ignore. We don't just go to church on Sunday and sit in our favorite pew and sing a few songs and go home. It's time to go to work for the Lord.

CHAPTER FIVE

Glory

The following is a letter that I wrote to Marks mom and his brother Stefan, Michelle, and Terry and Bobby Grapenthin, just a few days after the Redeeming of our Land. I can't thank them all enough, for being obedient to their calling in the Lord and for coming to us in our time of great need and desperation. They had the answers. I thank God for them.

I wrote to Mark's mom:

After you all left yesterday we had a great sense of peace. Mark went on to bed and so did Cassie and Rachel. I could lay upstairs on the bed with no fear at all. I didn't feel the need to constantly look over my shoulder. Mitch noticed the peace as well in his bedroom. It was true and total peace for the first time in our home. Praise the Lord. Thank you Jesus. We all slept well.

First thing this morning Rachel's friend who doesn't believe in God paid us a visit. His name is Mike. He pulled in the drive and I immediately thought, 'Oh no, I just got this house cleaned. What do I do now?'

As Rachel let him in, I began to pray that whatever was entering with him, that it be bound and that it could not have any connections to this house or us. His first question (since he had been told of our problems here and had seen the photo of the upstairs) was, "So did anything else happen? Any more ghost activity?" I went into the living room and I said to him that yes, some more had happened and that it was not good but evil. I told him it was gone. We had prayed and it had been bound up and had fled from here. He shifted a bit uncomfortably in his seat.

I said it is not here anymore. He said, "Well you said you prayed before and it didn't leave." I told him this time was different and that we took authoritative steps to rid our home of this. It had to leave us alone. He said, "Well, I don't feel the need to look over my shoulder anymore, but I think you should take some photos in the house to make sure." I said "NO. I am certain it is gone." He said, "You may need some proof." I said, "No, it is gone. It is over. We prayed it out. We blessed the house and the land. We will not allow it to be here any longer."

He said, "I think it's still here." (Right away I knew this was our first direct attack by Satan.) I stood firm and looked him in the eye. I kept praying "Lord through your power I bind those spirits and they can not come in here."

Rachel began to testify to him what had happened to her and

how she felt. He listened. Then he looked at me and said, "I always wanted to be a ghost buster. Why didn't you call me that night?" I said "Oh I should have! You would have been amazed at God's power at that time."

I watched him shift uncomfortably. I said, "You can take that feeling of wanting to do that and use it for God or for evil. The choice is yours." I began to tell him about the evil forces and spiritual battles that are around all of us. He listened and came back and sat down on the couch. Rachel began to tell him of her desire to go to the classes at your church. He said, "Hmmmm." I know that he doesn't feel anything in church he said, so he doesn't believe God is real. I told him, "It is amazing at how much I felt and how many churches do not teach this."

Rachel said "mom did you see his ring?" I had seen it. Boy had I seen it! I knew it was not good the minute he walked into the door. I felt it and my eyes went to the ring. By now Cassie was home from school and sitting with me. I kept praying to God to protect her from this because she had been through so much already. He said, "My ring is a black beam of light." He squeezed it and it shot out at Cassie and I put my hand up and said, "Don't." I said, "I see the ring." He said it lights up his room at night and is so bright. I kept praying inside that God protect us from that.

As I prayed, the ring literally began to fall apart. The top of it kept dropping off onto my floor. He said, "Wow, it keeps breaking. I wonder why? It never did that before!" PRAISE THE LORD. GOD

IS SO GOOD.

Finally he got up to leave and I reminded him that I am allowing only good in my house now and that he had choices to make on what he wanted to do with the interest he had in this. I knew he'd never been taught anything. That made me sad. We will keep him in our prayers.

As I tucked Cassie into bed last night, I looked down at her and I felt that there was still something in that room that needed to be found and thrown out. I looked down and there sat a little trinket box that had witch symbols painted all across it. I had remembered that box. I got it from Claire's in a surprise $1 gift bag. The minute I opened it, many months ago, I looked at Rachel and said I don't like that. But at the time, I didn't know that it meant what it meant. But it always bothered me. I found the lid to it on Sunday night and had thrown that out. But the box I could not find. As I tucked Cassie into bed... there was that box. Sitting without its lid right on the nightstand by her bed. I had searched there before and it wasn't there. I picked it up and felt instant nausea. I prayed "God I bind this spirit to this and it can have no more connections to this house or my children." I brought it downstairs and couldn't get it out of my hand fast enough to Mark. I said, "Here, this is bad. Real bad. Get it out. Pray over it and get it out."

He was reading and kind of ignored me. Then he looked down and said, "OH THIS IS BAD!" I said, "Get it out." He took it outside and when he came in, he said, "Sue that had the hairs on the back of my neck standing up." I said did you pray over it? He said the best he could. I prayed more. It was awful. Margo, it was awful. The minute it was out of Cassie's room I looked at her in her bed with her Faith and Hope prayer dolls all snuggled up and I had peace again. She looked so innocent and the room and the bed looked clean.

Steve, I bet you didn't know that as you all took those classes that you would be such a help to your own sister and your brother.

Margo, I bet you didn't know that as you prayed at the altar and took those classes that God would send you to your family in a prophetic dream in this time of need and that you would shortly arrive with spiritual armor on.

Michelle, I bet you didn't know that one day you would reach out and stop your sister in law from running out the door and hold my hands and take on the spirit of fear, face to face with me. You were so strong. You were all so strong.

Bobbi and Terry... I bet at one time you didn't know that one day you would save a family from total destruction. Your great guidance and leadership led the way to the Holy Spirit. You are awesome. God sent you to us specifically. I felt as though I'd known you when you walked into the door. You made us so comfortable instead of worried or ashamed. God Bless you all. We are so grateful to have been given this gift from God. We are waiting for God's instruction. We love you... Mark and Sue.

After writing this letter, I was approached just a few days later by a man in a restaurant. He was in line ahead of me while we waited to pay for our meals. He turned and looked at me and I said, "Long line today huh?" He said, "YES, it is." He said, "I'm not doing too good today." I said, "No?" He said no, I have to stand back and gather my thoughts up sometimes. See I was in a car accident and I went through the passenger side window of the car and I was in a coma for 3 months." I said, "Well, you look so good for having been through something like that." He laughed and said, "Well, when I came out of the coma I weighed 130 pounds and now I weigh 245!" and he patted his belly and chuckled. I said, "No, you look great." He said, "Well you know I died 5 times and they brought me back." I said, "My goodness." He said, "Well, I have the Holy Spirit you know!" Then he said, "You know about that, don't you?"

I was shocked. I said, "Isn't that great?" He said, "Three times and that's it." I said, "What?" He said, "Three times and that is it." He said, "The Holy Spirit called to me 3 times. The first time I ignored it. The second time I didn't listen. I served in the war and fought and had bullets fly past me as I lay in the bushes and nothing hurt me, but the car accident got me. The third time the Holy Spirit called, I listened." Then he said, "You go on ahead of me and pay. I need to stay back here and collect my thoughts awhile." I went on ahead to pay and when I turned around to leave, I said goodbye. I heard as I was leaving the woman at the counter say, "Sir can I help you? You've been waiting for so long there." He said, "No, I just need to wait here awhile." As I walked away, I had goose bumps. I believed it was a direct word from God that I needed to hear His calling and never turn back.

After leaving our home that night of redeeming the land, both of our families had the spirit of fear come upon them in the middle of the night and prayed it away. My mother in law received a phone call on her answering machine while they were at my house praying, that she said she knows was many demons screeching in the phone and screaming hideously. She said there were many, many of them. Many voices. We were told that Bobby was visiting someone and the phone rang there with the same screeching. They bound it up in the name of Jesus and today, before working in deliverance or redeeming of the land, they pray that there will be no manifestations over the phone. No longer are they bothered with the phone calls now. I'm so glad that we have a greater power in the Lord! These demons were angry with them for their help and prayers for us.

We were amazed at how quickly God had removed the scales from our eyes. We could literally see the good and evil in the world.

I began to realize that going way back to my childhood, when I was seeing so called "ghosts", that they weren't ghosts at all, but demonic presences that wanted me to be fascinated with the so-called "other side". When I saw these "ghosts" I was actually using a gift from the Lord, which was my ability to discern an evil presence and warn someone about it, but I didn't know it then. Satan was using these events and so-called "sightings" to detour my walk with God. This is also how many people get caught up in the dark side, wanting to see more. Do not seek the evil. It is a dangerous game to play. The Bible says in Amos 5:14, "Seek good, not evil, that you may live. So the LORD God of hosts will be with you."

When I sensed as a child that we shouldn't take a car trip to Arkansas that ended in a car accident, I was using a gift from the Lord. I just never knew how to use these gifts. Today I hear one story after another where God given discernment about a situation saved someone from harm or even death. I thank God for the way He speaks to us. It is a God given gift and ability. God was trying to speak to my family, through me that day.

When my son, Mitch, sensed that something bad was about to happen, and later my husband was involved in a car accident, that was a key time that my family should have gathered together and entered into prayer. Satan had a plan and if only we'd known what to do, when the warning came. We should have prayed and bound up every attack of the enemy against us and pled the Blood of Jesus upon us for protection. We should have gathered others to pray with us.

When I thought my grandmother had come into the room after her passing, well, that was not my grandmother. That was an evil presence seeking to deceive me.

When my first marriage failed, that was not his fault, nor my fault. It was the fault of satan who seeks to kill and destroy and these demons had some legal right to come into our lives and destroy us. I didn't have the knowledge back then of how to pray against it or remove it's legal right. How many marriages start out in sin? If you haven't followed God's law completely and don't repent and ask Jesus to forgive you and protect you, your marriage is at risk.

When illness and seizures came upon my daughter, it was again satan who seeks to kill and destroy. We don't have to live with illness. We carry the authority of Jesus Christ over that as well.

Satan wanted to destroy Mark and I, as well. He wanted us and he wanted our children. He knew our calling. He knew our gifts. Demons were sent to hinder us and to prevent us from ever realizing this. It is no different in the lives of countless others who will read this. Satan doesn't want you to find out your gifts in Christ Jesus.

We were invited to speak at my sister's church and tell a bit of this story. They prayed for us and we are so ready and so willing to do the Lord's work and share this. We want to help everyone who has ever felt the oppression of the evil forces that have at one time influenced us all. We have received word that this story has been sent out to many people in many other states who are throwing out their Harry Potter items and Pokemon things and Blessing and Redeeming their land and taking Communion in their houses. Praise God! Glory!

God comes in with a great force when you are ready to accept

Him and he blows the doors off of evil and he bombards their walls and breaks them down and they have no choice, no choice but to flee.

Mark and I now know that these are definitely the end times that we are living in. The Bible tells us about demons and God's power. We know in our hearts that these demonic forces are gaining in strength and numbers because their times are limited. Just as the forces in our home began to manifest and do more harm after I had the prophetic dream that help was on its way. They knew that their time was short and they were trying to destroy us quickly before that help got here, leading Mark to drink heavily and our little girl to fall mysteriously ill. I was just a few days away from leaving my husband when help arrived.

What we want to tell you more than anything is that the help that comes from God is far greater and stronger than anything else. It comes as a blessing of love and peace like you've never felt.

Our home and our lives were set free from evil in November of 2001. God worked quickly in our lives to show us His power. When God comes in and so quickly sets someone free, He begins to use you, immediately moving you into ministry. We've been caught up in a beautiful whirlwind that God created and we have found and seen His glorious power. He literally took us from terror to glory.

Within the first few months our story went out to churches and to others by email and we found ourselves pushed to the forefront of ministry.

Glory

A wonderful woman in the Lord, Janice Clark, came to our church to preach and minister in the prophetic to our congregation. It was the first time I would come to see this wonderful gift of the Lord. The first time she saw my husband and I walk through the door of the church she said she literally saw God pushing us, just pushing us, to the forefront of ministry. She said she saw us one day standing at the western wall in Jerusalem, weeping for the Jews that couldn't see or hear. It was amazing to hear God's plans revealed.

Janice began to share her testimony of gold dust appearing in her Bible and it literally appeared on the pages of her Bible as she began to preach the word of God. Janice had also had feathers fall from Heaven and diamonds. Yes, diamonds. Glory!

As Janice preached that night, gold flakes fell on us in our seats and appeared in our hands. We had it on our clothes and on our faces. Glory!

Many people have asked me why would God do such a thing? The streets of Heaven are paved with gold! It is nothing for God to bestow a gift like that on His children. Bobby once told me that in the Bible times, when a man was about to marry and take a bride, he would send over a gift of gold to her, to let her know that he was coming for her soon. It meant to get ready for the wedding. Bobby said Jesus is coming soon for His bride, the church. He is telling His people, His "bride" to get ready! She also explained it to me in this way. Our Father in Heaven loves His children and He loves bestowing gifts upon them and seeing their reactions to His miracles, signs and wonders, just as we too would enjoy seeing our own children get a gift that brought joy to their lives. He loves seeing our joy at His gifts! Glory!

One of the most amazing gifts we received from the Lord was the gold fillings in our teeth. A wonderful man, Phil Rich, who operates fully in the apostolic and prophetic, came to our church and while he was there, many received the gift of gold fillings. Marks mother, Margo received many gold fillings as well as a solid gold tooth. Margo came with me to a ladies meeting and prayed for a group of ladies to also receive this gift from God, and it was there that I too, received the gold in my fillings. We watched my sisters filling change to gold before our eyes! We came home so excited over what God had done and as we shared the story with Mark. We looked at his teeth and he too had the gold in his fillings. It was so wonderful to see this anointing spread. Glory!

The second time I came to witness the amazing gift of prophecy was when a couple came to our church, Harold and Kay Beyer. Kay prophesied over me, saying that the Lord, who loved me very much, had called me out of many years of darkness for a reason. That He knew it had been a long time, but that He planned it to be now that I would be set free. Glory!

Next Harold and Kay told their story of how God began to cause manna (a small cracker like substance that tastes of honey) to appear on their Bible. Manna was sent from God to sustain the people of Israel for 40 years while they lived in the wilderness.

(Exodus 16:35.) I was able to see the manna that literally fell from Heaven, saved in Harold's Bible. Glory!

Harold and Kay gave their testimony, sharing of how God had given them money numerous times. They had found it or come across it every time they needed it. Our God does provide! Literally! Glory!

How many people today spend money on a phone call to a psychic? They don't realize that they are going to someone who is delving into darkness and satans powers. Many are hungry for words of encouragement to uplift them and show them something about their future. They don't realize what an open door this is to allowing evil to come into their lives. I've heard many accounts of people going to a psychic and without realizing it, they are being cursed, with words spoken against their lives and they suddenly begin to see illness or bizarre accidents come upon them.

People are so hungry for the supernatural. It is a natural instinct within us that satan has tried to take advantage of. Desiring the supernatural is a God given emotion within us! OUR GOD IS SUPERNATURAL! Our God is also a jealous God and does not want us seeking words for our future through the devil or pagan religions or mysterious games or psychic's, or horoscopes, or tarot cards. He wants us to come to Him and Him only. He is the Way, the Truth and the Light.

Many churches today have stopped believing in miracles, signs and wonders. They believe it was for a time when Jesus was here, or in the Old Testament only. God didn't stop anything! God is still alive!

Some churches have removed God from the church. They've taken His power out of it. He is a God of great power! Satan had a plan to cause people to stop looking to God. He has principalities and powers and religious spirits over many of our churches today, binding them from seeing the actual hand of God. When people can't find God in the church, they sadly leave out of boredom. When people aren't told about God as He truly is, a God who loves them unconditionally, and instead a different image is portrayed, one of an angry and stern mean father figure, they are so uncomfortable that they begin to go look for something that is at least fun to them for a season. This is so sad to realize what has happened. When you come to know the Lord personally, and you see Him in His true and glorious light and love, you never look back or continue seeking anywhere else.

I'll never forget one day when we were worshipping at church. We were all singing and focusing solely on God and Jesus and praising and lifting our hands and singing out to Jesus, and I experienced my first vision. I saw Jesus. He was in a Jewish dancing pose with His hand raised in the air and He was looking over His shoulder at me and laughing joyously. He was weaving in and around and in between the people there and gazing in their faces and laughing and rejoicing with us. I painted Him after that. I tried to capture the look of joy and love and acceptance of all, on His face. My

Glory

painting hangs in my living room today.

If more people could only realize, God loves you so much. He sent His Son. His Son loves you. He died for you. The Lord does not condemn you, like many churches would have you to believe. Go back, after reading our story here and read the New Testament, where Jesus ministered to so many. Never did He say, "You've done so much wrong, that you don't have a place in My Father's Kingdom!" He didn't judge those people back then and He doesn't now.

God wants you to see His power, His love, His miracles, signs and wonders, and His glory! He wants you! It doesn't matter where you came from. It doesn't matter what you've done. All that He asks is that we repent and see Him now.

When His miracles, signs and wonders and His mighty power are allowed to work in a church, it is a power like no other. We've heard stories of witches and people of the occult purposely being sent out against churches to curse the church and these people have sat in our congregations to try and prevent God's power from coming forth. These people unfortunately have seen the power of satan work for them. Yes, satan too has power. However, I've also heard stories of people in the Lord who know their authority in Christ Jesus, who have seen His power, not being hindered by these witches at all. I've heard stories of witches coming up to them afterward and saying, "I want to serve the God you serve! I've stopped numerous people, but I can't stop you!" Our God is so powerful and even witches realize that satan's power is no match for God, when they are able to witness the trueness of what our God can do. Evil has been allowed to feel welcome in the house of the Lord. It's time to get satan back out and let the power of the Lord back in. God is awesome and amazing and waiting for all to come to Him.

We've had amazing opportunities in the Lord. We were quickly moved to the forefront of ministry. We've laid hands on the sick and seen them healed. We've heard angels sing in services and could even hear their angelic voices as we drove home after church some nights. We attended one service where it literally rained a Holy Rain from God in our church. The banners that hung from the ceiling became wet and the watermarks still remain there today. We've been in church services where we'll look down and there will be gold dust in our hands and on our clothing. We've seen angels such as glorious angels in gold and dancing angels and ministering angels. Glory!

We both went through deliverance through our church, Living Water Christian Fellowship. Our pastors have been involved in deliverance for years.

We all carry demonic presences that manipulate and control our day-to-day emotions. Some are there from doors we've opened in the past, through sin, that allowed them to come in. Some are there from our ancestors and passed on from generation to generation. Poverty for example could follow a family line and the children and children's children could be cursed. God will remove that and stop that curse in its tracks, if people knew how to renounce the sins of our forefathers and ask God to put a Jesus Christ bloodline of protection upon us. There can also be spirits of illness and infirmity and disease passed down to us as well. We wanted all of these things off of us. We wanted to be fully set free. We didn't want our children burdened with these things either.

A few days prior to our deliverance, we began to feel overwhelmed and unable to worship freely. These hindering spirits didn't want to go. We did homework to bring to attention and renounce the things of our past and our ancestors past and then met the pastor's at the church. I sat down opposite of Bobby and as she began to command these spirits to leave, an evil presence made itself known. I began to feel a large hand, with longer than normal fingers and chilling coldness, grasp my left shoulder and start pulling me away from her. I told her about this presence and she asked her daughter to place her hand over the area. Her daughter could feel the coldness as well. She then commanded the thing to leave me, in the name of Jesus. It had to go at that command. As it began to relax its grip, I felt this thing literally lift off of me. I felt it come up from within me. Chills began to run up and down my back and then move up to my neck and then a buzzing sound and tingling in my head as this thing peeled itself out of me. I remember thinking, 'Get off of me already!' and feeling relief as it did. There were a few other presences that left as well, as she went through the list of demonic strongholds.

After deliverance I felt like a new person. Mark did too. We both were able to worship God so much more freely. It was glorious! We were not hindered in any way. It was total freedom! Glory!

During the time that Glory was being revealed to us by God, Rachel, my oldest daughter, had moved into an apartment. She was planning to marry and Mark and I both questioned this relationship. I sensed evil around her fiancé and his family, but I knew for some reason that I needed to speak my concerns but also love him and bless this marriage. Rachel refused to listen to our advice and continued on with her plans. They had even talked of running away to marry, if I didn't give them my blessing. I decided to bless it and guide them.

Several weeks before the wedding, I began to notice that my daughter seemed distant. At her wedding shower, I had to remind her to say thank you, and that was very much unlike her. Her fiancé had attended church with us and had rededicated his life to the Lord. His desire to change was there, we thought.

Phil Rich, came back to our church and Rachel attended. She went up for prayer and Phil while laying hands upon her said, "Be made whole." He didn't know that she had a seizure disorder. Rachel felt touched by God that day, and she shared that she wanted to come off of her seizure medication. I asked her to wait and speak with her doctor.

She also went through deliverance with our pastors. They sensed though, that there were still some issues that she wasn't ready to let go of.

Rachel's next doctor appointment went well and they gave her the ok, to try and come off of her seizure medication. She slowly reduced the dosage until she was taking none.

During the fourth of July 2001 we had some wonderful houseguests staying with us from Vinesong, a wonderful group that travels and sings for the Lord, ministering to many. The family that stayed with us was from Nigeria. Bode and Yemesi and their daughter Rebecca.

The first morning that they were with us, I received a phone call from a distraught mother who said her son had stayed at my daughter's apartment the previous night. I told her that I'd go over and tell him that she wanted him home. I walked up the steps to Rachel's apartment and saw that the door was open and stepped inside. I began to hear a high pitched screeching, much like Margo had explained to me in regards to the phone call she had received. I looked around the living room and the sight was awful. These kids had been practicing witchcraft in my daughter's apartment and they were all there and her fiancé was leading much of it. To this day, I have a difficult time speaking of what I found. Her fiancé had a young man coming into the apartment and reading from his satanic books and there was a pentagram drawn on the back of the television. Many demonic pictures, that were samples of tattoos that they had been trying to place on each other. I have to leave other details out, but I can tell you with certainty, that Rachel confirmed for us that they had spoke incantations and spells over her. I believe they had gained some control over her thoughts and mind. She had willingly gone along with these things, but she didn't know the impact of what she had done. Her eyes had been blinded to the horribleness of it all.

When I discovered this, I looked at her fiancé and told him that this game was over. He came at me angrily and I walked out and called my husband and my ex husband. Working together, we removed all of our daughter's belongings and had her moved out within an hour. We shut the place down. Today, my husband and I rejoice over the fact that I was able to stay calm in spite of what I walked in on, and that we just calmly moved her out and closed it down. God was there for us and I knew it. He was leading me. I realized that more afterwards though than at that precise moment.

I can't tell you enough, how comforting it was to have Bode and his family with us in our home during this trying time. He lifted us up in prayer and prayed with us nightly. God knew the timing. He'd planned it. Glory!

I had asked my ex husband if he could take my daughter home with him for a while. He seemed so ready and willing to help and I was grateful. I met with his wife and we all worked together to try and help Rachel. I came to find out that his wife is a wonderful and loving woman and it's been a pleasure getting to know her. It was a huge healing in all of our lives. I was unable to communicate with my ex husband prior to this. Again, I knew God had His hand in it.

Glory

Even though evil seemed more apparent in Rachel's life at the time, God was working mightily. I kept lifting her up in prayer and so did the members of our church and our family.

Soon after finding Rachel like I did, I had the opportunity to travel to Virginia with Bobby to Calvary Pentecostal Campground. We stayed there on the campground for two nights and three days and I had such an amazing experience in the Lord. The first evening's service I was amazed at the freedom of worship. Everyone came with full expectations that the Lord would show up there. Armond Stevens was preaching that night and as the people worshipped I watched feathers appear mid-air and float downward. People would run up and catch them. The feathers were very fine and downy in appearance and different than any feather I had seen. I was told that they fall in many colors, some unlike any colors we've ever seen.

Next, a woman there had a diamond fall from heaven right in front of her. Bobby, being in the jewelry business for years, had her loop (or jeweler's eyepiece) with her. We had the opportunity to view this incredible diamond in our room that night. It was faceted on 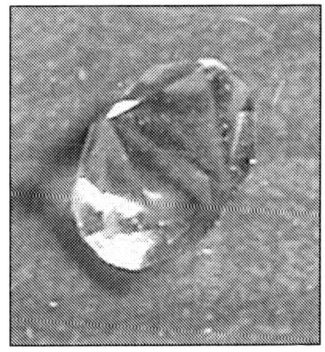 both sides. It was an amazing and miraculous cut that no man could re-create. It was gorgeous! Glory!

The second night there I had the opportunity to hear Silvania

Machado speak. She was a woman once very near death and God healed her at a church service. She was in pain for many years before God healed her diseased body. Since her healing, gold has been falling from her hair and oil comes from her hands. I was standing up front when she came forward and bent her head over and gold dust fell in a pile upon a Bible placed there. When you see God's glory like that, in that degree, all you can do is fall to your knees and weep. He is real. He is so real and while a joy came over me, I felt so sad that others don't recognize Him. I knelt and just wept.

A few minutes later as Silvania returned to her seat, and the music began again, everyone began to worship the Lord. I sat there on the floor praising God and praying to Him. I know at that moment it was as if there was only the two of us, God and I. I felt such closeness there, with Him and there was no other thought in my mind. It was as if warring angels had come down and pulled the thoughts away and held them at bay so that I could experience Him and His presence and His Glory! I lifted my hands up to Him and as I did, it began to rain gold dust. It fell like snow, only much finer and more of it. It sparkled in the light as it fell on me. I lifted my eyes and it wasn't coming from the ceiling, but it was appearing at my eye level and falling into my hands. On that night I had experienced His Glory like never before. Glory, Glory, Glory! I'll never forget it. Glory!

As Rachel began to pick up the pieces and begin again, she was very angry with me and shoved me away from her. She refused to come visit or to call me. The few times we did speak, I reminded her that satan was doing this and that he didn't want her to have a relationship with me.

Our pastors told us that this was an attack against the ministry that God was raising up in Mark and I. They also added that I had to let Rachel go for a while. Not so satan could have her, but so that God could. Those words carried me through.

One evening, weeks later Rachel surprised me by coming for a visit. She lingered with me quite a while. I just kept hearing God say, "Love her unconditionally, like I would." We never spoke much about the past, but had a nice visit. She returned the next night and the night after that.

One night while talking she shared with me that she'd been seeing a demonic presence around her. It was not pretty from the way she described it. We immediately called Terry and Bobby and they listened to her story and prayed with her. They shared with me that they truly felt it was an assignment of witchcraft sent against her, by her ex fiancé. They told us to pray with her, binding it up in the Name of Jesus and then all of us taking Communion. We did just that.

Rachel began to attend church with us again and this time, I witnessed her true and humble heart come forth as she worshipped and prayed to God. She was coming to the Lord on her own now. She was of age and He was telling me, "I have her now." He was waiting on her to want Him. Not just me wanting Him, for her.

One night while Rachel and I were walking, she again saw this demon standing in a field and staring at us. She yelled, "There it is again!" I looked in the direction she was pointing and I couldn't see it. However, I screamed, "Go! In the name of Jesus!" She said it flashed but was still there. Again I shouted, "I bind you up, in the name of Jesus Christ!" She said, "It's gone!"

As of the day I write this, my daughter Rachel hasn't been troubled by that evil again. GLORY TO GOD!

Phil Rich visited our church once again and Rachel shared with him of how when he'd laid hands on her, she'd felt healed and had wanted to get off of her seizure medication. She told him that to this day she has remained seizure free and medication free.

I shared that seizures weren't the only thing she had been set free of. God had set her free through the deliverance ministry of Terry and Bobby Grapenthin and Living Water Christian Fellowship as well. Phil was blessed to hear the testimony, as we all were. He prophesied over Rachel and said that her testimony was touching family. I said, "Yes!" Some of the family on my side and her father's side had never thought much of an evil presence and the way evil can come in and affect a life. They hadn't yet seen the gold dust or the glory we had all witnessed. They watched a dire situation in Rachel turn into an answer to prayers. They knew what God had done. GLORY!

A truly anointed couple, A.L. and Joyce Gill, who visit our

church on a regular basis, have greatly impacted and helped direc our walk with the Lord. Their wisdom and knowledge in the Lord, when shared, quickly raises a persons understanding of who God is.

Today, and it hasn't even been a full year yet as I write this, my husband and I work in the ministry in any way that God can use us. Since our story has gotten out about the house, we've been called to other homes to help them Redeem their land and help rid them of the evil that influences their homes. It's wonderful to see people who couldn't sleep in their house another night, learn their authority over evil and relax and be able to go to sleep that very same night in peace. God is so powerful and amazing. Glory!

Since we've all gained knowledge and insight in all of this, we can share with you that back when the seizures came upon Rachel a second time in life, it was because she opened the door. When we allow sin to overtake our lives and willfully go against what we know to be true in God, we put ourselves in dangerous territory. Especially when we have a high calling to work for the Lord.

Phil Rich shared that with us, during one of his visits to our church. Phil said if God calls you and you work for Him and then turn your back on Him, it's a dangerous place to be. He said that no longer will you see the glorious visions of God, but you'll begin to see the demonic instead. Rachel looked at me and I turned to look at her. It was exactly what had happened in her very own life. Thank you God, for bringing her back to You, and to us.

Rachel wrote her testimony down for Phil Rich and he said it would help many others when they hear it, that they too, can be set free of a horrible disease like seizures. Praise God. Look at the testimony! Glory!

Our daughter Cassidy is moving in the prophetic at a young age. We've watched her gather flags and scarves during worship and precisely place them where she feels God leads. We recently discovered that in the first grade, our daughter, who was once under such demonic attack that she was literally unexplainably ill, now writes prophetic words from God. While cleaning one day I found the following note, written by my six-year-old daughter. While some of it was misspelled, the message was clear… "When the rockets will blast and we will follow and the fireworks will shine, the night will go on and then the sun (son) will show on the world. Jesus." It was the best way a little girl could describe the rapture. God is working in her life quickly.

Today as we enter into prayer, gold appears on our hands and on our clothing.

At first it occurred only at church, and now it appears in our home, or in a restaurant while we are eating out after church. While witnessing to a young lady, in our dining room, it appeared, to her amazement on her clothing. While praying recently at 2 am, God caused a miracle of manna to appear on our Bible. Glory!

God has these gifts of miracles, signs and wonders and glory in store for you as well. He has it to offer to all, who come fully and expectantly to Him, leaving all things of the world behind. We've heard some comment that God's signs and wonders were for the Old Testament only, or that He just doesn't do things like this today. We've had some ask, "How do you know it is God?"

God is still God. He didn't change things, humanity did. People are uncomfortable knowing that He is "so real" that He would do this. Many are afraid. Satan would work in this way, to keep us from entering in, to God's Holy Presence, wouldn't he? I know it's our God producing these miracles. Satan wouldn't do something that would cause us such peace that we seek more of Jesus! Are there false gifts out there? Absolutely. How do we know the difference? They will never mention Jesus Christ where these false gifts abound, and they will never mention the Blood of Jesus, that was shed on the Cross for us. The Bible encourages us to test these things. We have tested them, and found them to be so true in Jesus Christ, that we fall to our knees and worship Him, thanking Him for His Glory.

Today, Mark and I both minister in worship at times and that in and of itself is an amazing story. I am not a keyboard player and Mark is not a guitar player but God moved and I am playing keyboard and he is playing electric guitar. Mark is a drummer though, and has been known to do spiritual warfare on the drums. Many have commented on how they see the Heaven's open as he plays and that they can hear hoof beats. Others have shared that they've had visions of chariots coming down out of heaven and a large army gathering. We have gone to the church to practice and God has given us brand new songs that very night to be played the next Sunday. God is moving so quickly that Mark and I joked that we wish He'd give us just a bit more time to practice. Glory! It's been amazing.

See, that is just it. God doesn't have time to give us the time. God needs people to work quickly for Him. We couldn't do it anyway, without Him. He is calling His people and He needs them to know about His love for them. Satan knows his time is limited and he has stepped up his powers. God is counter acting that and showing us His Glory! This is a battle for souls after all. God is so ready to pour out His power and He is just waiting for someone to realize that they are gifted in Him and He does still perform miracles.

May God bless you and continually enrich your lives. For those of you that haven't yet experienced His presence, for those of you who see things that are causing you fear, for those of you that may feel down or depressed and don't know why you can't shake that feeling off, for those of you that can't sleep at night in your own home, for those of you that struggle with alcoholism and other addictions, for those of you that feel bound and unable to find peace and contentment... Lord touch them now, in Jesus' Name... and let them too, find the way from Terror to Glory.

If you don't know Jesus:

If you haven't come to know the Risen Savior, Jesus Christ, personally, then please allow me to introduce you to Him. He is a glorious and loving God and He has been waiting for you! He has had a plan in your life, to bring you to this point in time, where you would cry out to Him. He will set you free. He will give you peace. Believe in Him. He is real and alive! Acts Chapter 10, verse 43 says, "To Him all the prophets witness saying that, through His name, whoever believes in Him will receive remission of sins."

Say this prayer, "Lord, forgive me of my sins. I believe in You and I want to be set free of the demons that are trying to destroy me. I'm sorry I didn't look to You, Lord. I'm sorry I sinned against You. Come into my heart Jesus and I know and I believe that I will be set free! I want to serve You Lord. Show me the way. Amen."

God Bless you! My heart rejoices, as do all of the Heavens! When you seek Him, he definitely takes you out of terror and puts you in His Glory!

LaVergne, TN USA
18 August 2010
193667LV00001B/71/A